The Herrs

by Mabel Burkholder

Conestoga Bookstore
2175 Division Highway
Ephrata, PA 17522
Ph. 717-354-0475 ● Fax 717-355-0709

Masthof Press
219 Mill Road
Morgantown, PA 19543-9516

THE HERRS

Illustrated by Anita Burkholder

All the characters in this book are historical figures who lived in these places in these times with the exception of two or three persons whose full names are not used.

Library of Congress Control Number: 2002114172
International Standard Book Number: 1-930353-69-3

Published 2003
Masthof Press
219 Mill Road
Morgantown, PA 19543-9516

Dedication

This book is dedicated to the ministers of my childhood whose stories of those who suffered and were persecuted, even unto death, sparked my interest in their history and faith.

Also, to my husband, Enos, whose many reminders of my promise to Amos B. Hoover to write their story for teenagers and adults has at last been fulfilled.

Steinsberg Fortress
Steinsberg, Germany

CHAPTER ONE

There was a smile on Christian Herr's face as he guided the oxen and cart out the road. He took one look back at the Unterbiegelhof where his parents, Hans and Elizabeth Herr, and their family lived with several other families.

It was 1698 and Christian felt pleased and quite grown up. This was the first time that Father had trusted him to take the wheat to be ground into flour at the mill along the Neckar River. He thought of Father's parting words.

"Mind your business now and be sure you don't do anything that will annoy any of the local people," reminding Father.

Christian nodded to himself. All of his young life, that was the warning Anabaptist boys were given. The local ruler and some of the local people had invited the hard-working "Swissers" to help rebuild and reclaim the land destroyed in the terrible Thirty Years War. Now some eyed their land and *hofs* and fertile fields with covetousness and resentment.

As the oxen slowly plodded along at their steady pace, Christian had lots of time to think. He thought of his brothers. Abraham was the oldest and would soon be married to Anna, his betrothed. That was one reason he'd been given the job to go to the mill today. Father and Abraham were working on tools for Abraham in the blacksmith shop on the *hof*. With several families sharing the same shop, they had to use it when it was available. And then there was his brother Hans, and his younger brothers, Emanuel and Isaac.

After crossing the first hill, he looked ahead in the distance to the Steinsberg on the right. Christian saw the hill and fortress that dominated the landscape for miles around. The Lutheran von Venningen family lived there and owned a great deal of land. Nearly fifty years ago, Father had told him, back in 1650, the von Venningens had invited several Swiss families from Zurich who were living in Alsace to settle here. In 1672, some Bernese families had also come.

His thoughts drifted to the mill. It was always interesting to watch the mill, thought Christian, no matter how often he'd seen it before. Many times Father had given him a task he'd thought too big and then said, "If you do it well, you may go along to the mill the next time." Christian always tried to do his best so that he would be able to go with Father to the mill.

While the wheat was being ground, Christian unhitched the oxen and gave them water and let them eat a bit of grass.

After the cart was loaded, Christian looked up once more at the Steinsberg. The fortress and the walls around it were certainly old, some said 500 years or more. Built before the year 1200, it had been destroyed several times during the days of the knights. The von Venningen family were knights and the people living around them were serfs, Father had said, which was almost the same as slaves.

Christian was approaching the village of Weiler, but was thinking of what life as a serf might have been like. The tower in the center of the Steinsberg rose high above the walls surrounding it. Those walls were probably six to eight feet thick, Christian thought.

"WHOA! WHOA! *Du–du dumphkop!*" (You blockhead). All of a sudden, Christian became aware that another large cart load of wheat pulled by two horses was at the opposite end of the narrow street he was on. Too late he remembered how Father always watched ahead in the distance to see if another cart was approaching.

With oxen yoked at the neck, they could pull but not back up. He knew that with horses it would be possible to back up, yet he also knew that **here** he was expected to yield. He was the one to unhitch the oxen, unload the cart, and turn it around, and then reload it and go outside the village until the other cart had passed. Father's words rang in his ears. "Don't do anything to annoy the local people." Now, by his carelessness and daydreaming about the hard life of a serf, he'd done just that. Maybe he wasn't as grown up as he'd thought this morning when he'd started off for the mill.

That evening at supper when Father asked how the trip to the mill had gone, Christian sheepishly and a bit haltingly related the problem he had caused. Father smiled. "You learned a better lesson than any I could have taught you."

"You know, I wondered today which of the Swiss brethren *hofs* one could see from up on top of the Steinsberg," questioned Christian.

Father nodded and replied, "Quite a few. There's the *hof* of the Biers, the Freys, Kauffmans, Landis, and Kendigs. Then there's the Musser, Meyer, Nussli, and Oberholtzer *hofs*. There's Rosenberger, Ruth, Hegi, Harnisch, and Hauser. Let me see, who did I miss," said Father as he counted them over again on his fingers. "There's the Sauters and I don't believe I said the Funks either. I'm not sure if I missed any or not. But if I'm not mistaken, all of those could be seen from the Steinsberg. Yes, the Steinsberg can be seen for miles, and if you were to go to the top of the tower, you could see for miles in every direction," Father said.

CHAPTER TWO

Christian Herr awoke with a start. Had he heard something? Or was it only his imagination? Yes, there it was again. The soft knocking at the door. Quickly he went towards his parents' room.

"There is someone at the door!" called Christian.

Christian's mother, Elizabeth, came from the bedroom and went to the fireplace to poke at the fire. She added more wood as Christian's father, Hans, went to the door, and lifted the latch.

"Brother Hans," a clear voice said from the shadows, "it's Benedict Brechbühl from Bern, Switzerland."

"Yes, yes, Benedict, come in," said Hans, stepping aside. "We had heard you might be coming." The men greeted one another with the holy kiss.

Mother swung the pot of water over the fire and reached for the linen cloth containing her bread. She sliced some bread and also set out some cheese. Getting a pitcher of milk, she filled an earthenware mug. Benedict must be hungry after his long journey.

The men talked quietly so as not to awaken the rest of the family, but young Hans, Christian's brother, had heard the noise for he came to the kitchen, too.

"Christian and Hans, go get the small bed tick and my cloak so we can make a bed by the fireplace." Mother asked softly as she sliced more bread.

As the boys arranged themselves near the fireplace, Mother went back to bed, leaving the door slightly ajar. Benedict Brechbühl was a zealous Swiss preacher from near Eggiwil in the canton of Bern, and she had heard much about him. His arrival meant there would be preaching services tomorrow evening. The boys would have to spread the word tomorrow. She could hear her husband and Benedict talking, and wondered if there was new trouble in Switzerland which meant that the Brethren may again face more persecution.

When all had quieted down and Christian had returned to bed, he lay and thought for awhile. It was the fall of 1700, and his mind wandered back to Switzerland where Father and Mother, as well as many other local Anabaptists, had been born. Now they lived in the Kraichgau, an area of the Palatinate in Germany, often called the Pfaltz.

Because Anabaptists do not bear arms or go to war and also practiced believers (adult) baptism, they were severely persecuted in Switzerland, as well as in Holland, and the surrounding countries. The Catholic Church called them heretics, and the Protestant Churches called them law-breakers.

Some people called the Anabaptists *Täufer* (rebaptizers); and here in Germany some still called them "Swissers." Because of the writings of Menno Simons, some had also started calling them *"Mennonisten"* (Mennonites).

Because they had been persecuted, Anabaptists had to take land other people didn't want. They even learned how to drain swamps to produce fields. Others learned to make the best use of mountain land by grazing cows (to make butter and cheese), and working hard to cut the summer mountain grass with a scythe for hay to give to the cattle to eat in the winter months. Over the winter, other farmers fed straw to their cattle, and they did not thrive as well as the cows who ate the sweet-smelling hay. Making hay was very hard work and required the help of the whole family. Christian well remembered his mother saying how important she'd felt once she was old enough to handle the large wooden rakes that the women used to rake the hay in piles. Then they would put the hay on large, rough woven cloth and put it on their backs to carry down the mountain.

It was because of their reputation as good farmers and their willingness to work hard that the Anabaptists were invited to the Palatinate after the terrible destruction of the Thirty Years War. Father and Mother still sighed deeply as they recalled the sight that had greeted them after the long, tiring journey on foot from Switzerland. The burned-out buildings, often just the blackened stone walls, were all that were left of what had once been houses and barns. The fields were overgrown with weeds, brush, and young trees because at least half of the residents, and in some places more than half, had been killed during the terrible war. No wonder they had been invited by the Elector Count Karl Ludwig to come and rebuild the houses and barns and restore the land before it was completely overgrown.

Those first years had been such hard ones. Several families would live together in crowded conditions while the houses were being rebuilt. Mother still talked of how her faith was tested during those hard times. But they also had learned some lessons of working together, and felt God's blessings after the little irritations had faded away.

With a sigh of his own, Christian rolled over and waited for sleep to return. The morning, with its responsibilities, would soon arrive.

The next day Benedict helped with the turnip harvest while Christian's younger brother, Emanuel, went to tell the neighbors there would be a meeting after dark at the home of Hans Herr. Mother didn't help with the turnips today; she had other things to do. Butter needed to be churned, the house needed a good cleaning, and the boards that were used for benches needed to be scrubbed.

In the evening when everything was ready, Christian sat beside Mother in the corner on the little three-legged stool and mentally counted as again and again the door opened. How many would come? A meeting of more than twenty people was forbidden; and getting caught might mean a heavy fine—a fine they didn't have the money to pay. If more than twenty came, he would have to inform one of the other boys to serve as a lookout. He sighed. That would mean that he would have to miss the sermon, but the neighbors had had to sell a heifer in order to pay the fine the last time, and he did not want his family to do that. He recognized the voice of his eldest brother Abraham among the recent arrivals and soon saw Abraham's wife Anna with baby Abraham. Once again the door opened. That was nineteen now. He waited a little longer, and when Mother went to check the fire, he sighed with relief.

The people were seated and Hans announced the song they would sing. Soon the words of the song *"O Gott Vater, wir loben dich, und deine Güte preisen; die du, O Herr, so gnädiglich an uns neu hast bewiesen,"* rose in praise, with Benedict leading in a clear bell-like voice. What a difference it made in the singing. Hans preached first, but he kept his words few. Then it was Benedict's turn. He had been baptized at twenty years of age, but only last year he had become a minister. Christian's heart burned within him as Benedict preached boldly from the Scriptures.

The next day, the Herrs worked on their turnip harvest, but quit early so that Hans and Benedict could hold another meeting that evening. Many times in the next months, Christian's thoughts returned to

Benedict Brechbühl and his stirring sermons, and he would frequently thank God for his visit.

*   *   *

Another war broke out! It was 1701 and the French soldiers once more made forays through the Swiss valleys. What would happen next wondered Father and Mother as they talked of twelve years earlier when French soldiers had marched through, leaving a path of fire and destruction. The boys were spellbound as their parents told of cities, villages, and even the castle of the ruler himself ruined as the torch was put to houses, barns, and grain. Nearly half of the 400 Swiss Brethren along with the local people had lost their homes. Mennonites of Holland had given money to help rebuild the houses. Some of the Brethren had escaped destruction by fleeing to the small islands in the Rhine River. There they built small huts from branches and straw and lived on whatever could be found, even frogs and snakes.

"Frogs and snakes!" exclaimed the Herr boys.

"Yes," said Father forcefully. "Our family had gone to the mountains and there were times when we'd have been only too glad to have a frog or snake to fill our hungry stomach."

*   *   *

In 1703, Benedict Brechbühl sent a letter to the Brethren in the Kraighgau area. He told them that last year he and his wife had a daughter, Maudlin; and this year, they had a newborn son named Ulrich. Benedict wrote that things were still unsettled in Bern. New *Täufer* hunts kept turning up and Hans Reist was expelled.

"But," he wrote, "the hunts aren't always successful. The neighbors protect us by blowing their Alp horns or shooting a gun to give us warning. There is even talk of shipping us over the ocean, so far from Bern and Zurich that we can never return. And they are not even content to stop with the *Täufer*." Samuel Guldin was the pastor of the *Grossmunster*, the largest Reformed Church in Bern, and they were not pleased with his preaching or Bible studies; so he too was exiled.

Father and Mother read Benedict's letter again and again; and as soon as the adult children arrived home, it was discussed more.

"You know," said Christian, "when the Brethren first moved here after the war, when the land was empty and everything burned out, we felt perhaps things might be better here. But after the destruction in 1689 and now during the new war, perhaps we should think of moving to America or somewhere else."

"Oh, but it's so far and the voyage is so dangerous. Besides, the Mennonites of Holland have helped us out so often already, just as they did when many lost their homes in '89," answered Father. "And anyone who left would know that they would be parting forever from friends and family here on earth."

*   *   *

One fall day in 1704, Christian Herr's brother Abraham sent word that their baby, Barbara, was seriously ill. Mother got her bags of herbs and roots and took Christian with her to Abraham's house. There she brewed some elderberry blossoms for tea. Mother washed Barbara's hot face and arms, and then spooned tea into her mouth. Christian split some wood while the women did what they could for baby Barbara.

"Please fetch me a handful of mint tea," Mother instructed Anna.

Twisting and turning and bruising the leaves, she put them into a small white linen cloth. Twisting the linen till drops of tea fell on the spoon, she gave it to the feverish baby, then she twisted it again. Six-month-old Barbara puckered her face but swallowed the tea. Once more Mother washed the fevered baby's face and hands. She also applied fried onions on her chest as a poultice. Then she rocked Barbara in the cradle. The baby kept whimpering but eventually fell asleep. Each time the child awoke, Mother reapplied the remedy.

Meanwhile, Christian played with the four boys: Abe, Rudolph, Christli, and baby Hans. When Mother was ready to leave for home, she and Christian walked home together in the soft light of the setting sun, praying for little Barbara as they walked. The mountains in the distance gave a feeling of peace as they gazed at them. Yes, baby Barbara was in the hands of God.

*   *   *

News drifted back to the Herr family of new persecutions in Bern in the fall of 1708. Christian had gone on an errand for Father when one of the Brethren stopped him on his way home.

"Here are some letters from Switzerland that your father and mother might like to see. They may read them and then pass them on further south of you." Christian quickened his steps, eager to hear what was happening.

Father unfolded the letters and read, "Table-maker Benedict Lehman, renter of a hill farm along the Emme River, had hidden for a year, Anna, wife of preacher Hans Gerber. Hans would visit there and hold services. On one such visit they were caught and both put into prison. Lehman was exiled for three months."

The next bad new was that Benedict Brechbühl and his wife, plus a number of other *Täufer* were exiled to Basel.

Mother sighed and commented that this was the second time that Benedict had been expelled. He had stayed with the Brethren at Mannheim for a time but soon returned, holding secret meetings again. He had said, "Why shall we stop meeting together to worship for the sake of man-made laws?" But then his neighbor, who knew where Benedict was hiding, refused to tell the authorities and consequently had to pay a heavy fine.

The angry officials in Bern now offered good rewards for catching *Täufer* leaders and had arrested Deacon Hans Burke that way. Earlier in the summer, Hans, his wife, and two sons had moved to a hut in the mountains, but he had given a meal to a poor man who then went to the officials in order to obtain the reward. Hans was put in the prison tower at Trachselwald where he became quite ill due to the cold surroundings. After a month in solitary confinement, he was taken to a prison in Bern known as "The Island."

A neighbor arrived one day with an update on Benedict Brechbühl, and said that Benedict and Verena Brechbühl were making plans to move to Mannheim, but early on the morning of January 12, 1709, they were frightened to see a constable with seven men heading for their farm.

Quickly trying to think of a place to hide, Verena said, "The haystack!" After helping her husband crawl in covering him up to make the hay look as if it hadn't been disturbed, Verena returned to the children.

Soon the eight men ransacked the house, opening chests, and looking through everything; searching in every nook and corner, but not finding Benedict. Then they tried the stables. Verena felt as if her heart would stop as she saw them poking their swords into the haystack again and again.

"Aha! He's in there!" shouted one.

Slowly the hay moved as Benedict crept out. At once they seized him.

"What's your name?" asked a man roughly.

"Are you a preacher?" shouted the constable.

Slowly Benedict nodded. There were shouts of glee at this news, because *Täufer* preachers brought double the reward price. The constable took Benedict into the house, boxed him on the ear, and tied his hands behind his back. Then he took him out the door.

Seeing this, the children (Maudlin, age seven, and Ulrich, age five) started screaming so loud that Verena thought it must surely melt a heart of stone. But the men acted as if they did not hear it and went down the mountain. Verena watched them as long as she could see them, feeling as if her heart would break with every step they took.

"Father, forgive them for they know not what they do," she prayed as the tears fell. She tried to comfort her heartbroken children. Later she was to learn that several of the men had been criminals who had been released from jail to come and help arrest Benedict. At first, that was one more bitter blow; but then she remembered that Christ, too, had been between criminals and had opened the door of heaven to one of them.

The Herr family shook their heads as they listened to the neighbor continue.

Ten days later, Benedict was in the prison known as "The Island" at Bern; in a dungeon where he was to spend four and a half months in leg irons checked every morning and every evening. The dungeon was shared with several others and because of the severe cold, they were permitted to have heat, but only if the prisoners themselves paid for the wood. Since Benedict's property had been seized in order to pay the rewards, there was no money for wood, let alone take care of his family.

The thought of the leg irons was very hard for Verena to accept, yet she knew how often the *Täufer* had escaped from prisons and dungeons. Benedict's spirit was not broken. He wrote a 160-line poem which began with these first two lines:

The one who wrote this little song, and for the first time sang it,
He lay at Bern within a jail, there to a chain enshackled.

After eighteen weeks in the dungeon, he was sentenced to a workshop called a hospital, where he joined fifty other *Täufer* including Deacon Hans Burke and Preacher Shenk. He was there for eight months. He and the other prisoners were fed only bread and water and had to work at cleaning and carding wool from four o'clock in the morning until eight o'clock at night. Very few visits were permitted.

On April 17, 1709, the Council of Bern made the decision that the *Täufer* were to be shipped into exile, either to the East or West Indies, or else to Pennsylvania.

A former Bern city councilor, Franz Luis Michel, had made contact with William Penn about settling a colony of Swiss people in Pennsylvania. Arriving in Philadelphia, Michel was much surprised at the growth and bustle of the new city, the many building projects under construction, and the very un-European liberty he found.

Six miles north of Philadelphia, Michel found Germantown and felt at home when he met several Swiss who had lived north of Bern. Michel explored Pennsylvania with Martin Chartier, a French Catholic who had explored the Mississippi region and had married a Shawnee Indian woman. He lived in an Indian village near the Susquehanna River, just above the place where the Pequea flowed into the Susquehannna. Michel was seeking rich silver mines and hoped the Indians would help him find them. So great were his hopes and dreams about the silver mines that on his return trip he was able to beguile William Penn with his tall tales so that Penn believed that these mines were even now operating. Penn, beset with debt, was hoping to find a way out. Favorable to Penn was a bill passed by the British Parliament, allowing the naturalization of foreign Protestants. This would mean that the German and Swiss people would find Pennsylvania a more attractive place to settle.

Unfortunately, Penn's troubles were far from over. In fact, they had just begun. On his way home from a meeting for worship, the well-known Quaker was arrested and put into debtors prison. His former agent, Philip Ford, who had managed Penn's estates, had managed to cheat him. He had learned that Penn signed papers without checking them, and kept the books so that it showed that Penn was greatly indebted to him. His widow had now pressed the suit. There was a court trial and Penn lost. From the debtors prison, Penn found the treachery almost unbelievable. True, it was not his first time in prison. He had been imprisoned several times for his Quaker beliefs and writings, once even in the tower of London. Yet here was a man who had been granted 29,000,000 acres—sitting in debtors prison. After several months, Penn finally mortgaged his whole colony to several wealthy Quaker businessmen to get out of prison. He was released on October 8, 1708.

*   *   *

Not only were the Swiss Brethren in the Palatinate in dire need, but their neighbors were also experiencing hardships. For three years, the roving French troops plus extra war taxes had taken a heavy toll. A Lutheran pastor, Joshua Harrsch, who had Swiss Brethren neighbors, such as Eby, Bomberger, Herr, Landis, Musselman, and Rohrer, traveled secretly to London. Queen Anne of England was a strong Protestant and Harrsch hoped to find help in London to send a colony to Carolina. He wrote an eighty-page booklet telling of the open, unspoiled country, where there were almost no taxes—the beautiful Carolina.

"Hardly any taxes!" said the people in the Palatinate. It was almost unbelievable. "Why, here we have taxes and more taxes. And as soon as we are almost on our feet from one war, along comes another war."

In March 1708, this pastor once again stole secretly away, leading a group of poor Lutherans down the Rhine River to Rotterdam and then to London. Here they were welcomed as spiritual heroes from the war with Catholic France. Once more this Lutheran pastor reprinted his booklet of the wonderful land in the Carolinas, adding an appendix, telling of what wonderful help they had received all along the Rhine and even in London itself.

The Lutheran group were shipped, not to Carolina, as they had hoped, but instead to New York. There they were to pay for their passage by producing tar and pitch for the British Navy.

*   *   *

Christian Herr tried to remember how the Brethren in Bern were being imprisoned and how often Mother and Father talked and prayed for them, but he did not know what to think. He thought back about eight years earlier to the visit of Benedict Brechbühl and about all he had heard since then about the sufferings of his family and friends. His brother Hans had gotten married a number of years ago and now they had three small children. Hans felt they should go to Carolina, especially after hearing about the booklet *Reports of the Famous Country of Carolina Situated in English America*. He and several other Brethren kept talking about it, but that was as far as it got. Just talk, at least as far as the Brethren were concerned.

The winter of 1708-9 turned bitter cold; colder than any of the old people could ever remember. Christian was sure he would never forget it as long as he lived. For many, it was a struggle just to keep their cattle alive and their family from freezing. Whole families moved in together, hoping to have enough wood to at least keep one hearth burning to melt ice for the cattle to drink. Cattle dung was mixed with straw and used to make the barns tighter. The frost on the inside from the breath of the cattle became very thick. Even the turnips froze in some of the root cellars.

When at last spring came, it seemed as if the very flood gates of immigration let loose. Hans wanted to go too, yet none of the other Brethren were ready or willing to go along.

One afternoon while Christian was out in the fields with the oxen. he saw Hans motioning from the edge of the field as if something were wrong.

"Do you want the land I'm farming, Christian? Frances and I are planning to leave for Rotterdam as soon as we can get ready," said Hans breathlessly, "that is, if Father and Mother approve. I just heard that a group of Brethren from further down the Rhine left and plan to sail for America soon," Hans continued.

Christian took a deep breath, too stunned at first to think clearly. Then he unhitched the tired oxen and tied them to a tree where they could eat grass. Then he walked back to the barn where Hans and Father were already talking.

"Who is going," asked Father, "and where are they from?"

"They are a group of Brethren from west of the Rhine River around Worms and Frankenthal, some say, around nine or ten households. One is the younger brother of elder Peter Kolb of Mannheim; his name is Heinrich Kolb, if I have it right. Three of his brothers left two years ago for Pennsylvania. I think they were Jacob, Martin, and

Johannes Kolb. There is also a Gerhart Clemens and a Marcus Oberholtzer. One of them also mentioned something about a ten-year-old boy, Jacob Groff, whose parents are already living there."

"When did these people leave and how will you meet up with them?" asked Father. By this time, younger brothers, Emanuel and Isaac, and Mother had also joined them and Hans had to tell his story again.

"What if you can't find them?" asked Mother.

"Will you promise to come back if you don't hook up with a group of our own faith?" Father asked.

"Whatever you do, don't go someplace where there are no others of the faith," admonished Mother.

Hans nodded, "Yes, I'm sure Frances would feel the same way."

"And if it's half as good as it sounds, get word back to us so we can come, too," added Christian.

"It's almost dinnertime," said Mother. "We'll be over to help as soon as we've eaten."

There was rye porridge and beets and fresh watercress for dinner. Oh, how glad the Herrs were for the fresh greens after the long winter. Had they not carefully hidden some rye from the French soldiers, there might not have been any grains left at all. The wheat was long gone. And how they all looked forward to one of the cows freshening soon, so that there would once more be milk, butter, and cheese. The cows that had been giving milk had stopped once it was so cold for so long. This winter of 1708-9 would always be remembered — not only in the Palatinate, but all over Europe — as "The Cold Winter." Whole herds of animals had died, trees and grape vines had frozen, and the Rhine River which flowed at fourteen miles an hour had frozen over too.

A few days later, Christian led the oxen with the cart packed with their possessions, some food, and the three children, while Hans and Frances walked with him. They paused only long enough to look up at the Steinsberg, the landmark fortress on the mountain in the distance; then they headed west to the Rhine River.

Even Christian caught some of the excitement in the air and yet he couldn't help but think back to the sober group at home as they'd given each other the holy kiss and said, *"Gott sie mitt euch!"* (God be with you). It was so sudden, so abrupt. Christian looked at the children—little Hans, Fanny, and baby Anna—already sleeping in the cart since they had started before dawn. How sweet and innocent they looked. They had no idea what was ahead of them. Actually, none of them knew what was ahead of them.

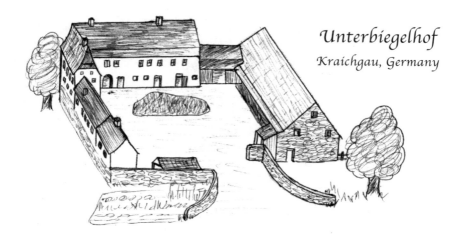

Unterbiegelhof
Kraichgau, Germany

Chapter Three

All summer long Christian Herr and his family prayed and wondered about the younger Hans Herr family. Isaac and Emanuel kept asking if their older brother had found the others. All spring and summer, many local people were leaving. With the war, the taxes, and then the long, cold winter, they had had all they could take. Reports said that Queen Anne of England, a staunch Protestant, had sympathy for the emigrants and was willing to pay their way to America. Her offer was hard to resist.

Many a night Christian would wake up and think of Hans and Frances and their three children. Were they on the ocean by now? What of the storms . . . the pirates . . . French warships? What hardships would they meet once they got there? Had they found the Brethren? Were they living?

Mother noticed that Christian wasn't sleeping well and questioned him.

Soon all Christian's worries came out. "It's this not knowing . . .
I think that's what's getting to me. Of course, sometimes I may be
waking up because they need prayers. I think surely they would have
been back by now if they had missed the group. . . . Not knowing makes
it so hard."

"Christian, I believe they do need our prayers, but I also wonder
if you don't need some more of the all-trusting and yielding faith the
old people called *Gelassenheit* (yieldedness). It's the same thing that
sustains us when the soldiers come and take our grain. We have trusted
that God would make a way—one way or another if we yield our all—
and He has!"

Christian nodded, "You are saying that the nonresistance we put
into practice then was a yielding . . . and this is just a different form of it.
It's trusting that God knows and cares, but yet we must yield to whatever
is His will for us . . . even if it goes against all our wants and wishes."

Mother nodded. "I wonder if those who do not learn this lesson
ever have true peace that doesn't swing with the wind."

During the next weeks as Christian worked long hours on the
wheat harvest, his mind returned again and again to Mother's words.
Soon he was sleeping better again. Hans and Frances and the children
were certainly in God's care.

The wheat they were harvesting was also in God's care. The Herrs
had survived other years in spite of the soldiers' raids. He thought of
Anna Bare, a girl of deep faith who was extra special to him. But,
Christian had to postpone once again the thought of marriage when his
family had barely enough to live on themselves, and certainly no land
or house available.

One night in early October, Christian felt he must be dreaming
when he thought he heard Hans speaking in the house. Oh—but yes,
that **was** Hans speaking! Quickly he jumped out of bed, waking Emanuel
and Isaac. "I hear Hans in the kitchen!" he said as he dressed in the
biggest hurry in a long time.

"Hans, Hans!" Christian and Hans clung to each other as they
gripped each other's hand for a very long time. As the other boys came
tumbling down the stairs, Hans said, "We missed them. . . missed them
by only a few days. But, it took awhile till we found out. We set sail
from Rotterdam on June 21, bound for London. Had we but known it,
the rest of the Brethren left London on June 24. Oh, it was quite a blow
to miss them by so little. But there were Palatines by the hundreds

everywhere in Rotterdam. Once we arrived in London, they were there by the thousands! I never saw so many people.

"When the Palatine refugees first arrive in Rotterdam, they are met with sympathetic help by Dutch officials; as well as the Mennonites who also gave us aid. In London it was the same way. The British secretary in Holland allowed us to sail to London at the Queen's expense. There in London, crowds came and stared at us poor Palatines; even the Queen came. Quakers came with shoes, Bibles, and Quaker booklets. However, as thousands more came, as many as twenty-eight to thirty people were housed in one room. The hotels and even a warehouse were overflowing, so Army tents were brought out and soon sprouted up almost overnight, much like mushrooms. It was a huge refugee city with only refugees. These refugee cities grew wherever there was open space along the Thames River or the Blackheath.

"We lived in a tent along the Thames for awhile until I finally found out for sure that the ship had sailed," Hans told them. "Soon there was talk that the Queen was going to send the Catholic families back. The bill that William Penn's friends had put through was only for foreign Protestants to become naturalized citizens. The Catholics were to be sent back. We had to arrange to come with them. But there were so many people, some say as many as 13,000. We never thought it would take so long.

"We were befriended by Quakers who told us their people had given £50 to fourteen Mennonite families who had sailed on June 24. That's when we found out how close we came to missing them. But even so, with so many people everywhere, we might have been there and missed them. It was the end of September before we could finally set sail back to Holland and up the Rhine.

"In the meantime, we worked for Quaker farmers outside London. When we saw how much sickness and death there was in the tent cities, we asked the Quakers if there wasn't some place in the country where we could go and work for our food until the ship would leave. Frances helped with the milking and butter-making and I helped to repair buildings. We even had our own garden which was a big help. We had a lot of late cabbage planted. The English had turnips, carrots, and parsnips, and some cabbage. It usually rains every day there, and the summers are cooler than here; but they told us that winters are not as cold there as here in Germany.

"But I still think we should organize a whole group from here and go to America. I'll need the cart and oxen to pick up Frances and the children who are staying with a family near the river."

Once Christian was back in bed, sleep would not come. Hans' stories kept circling around in his head like bumblebees. The hopes of a whole group going . . . he thought of Anna, his betrothed. They had hoped to get married in the winter even if they had to live with his parents. What would she say . . . would she be willing to go?

Since several of the Brethren had read the booklet about the Carolinas, some were interested in going there.

In the next days and weeks, Christian was surprised at how much interest was shown in America. Now that Hans had gone to London and returned, it seemed wherever one of them went, there were questions asked, some of which they could answer and many more that they could not.

Mother's brother, Martin Kendig, was interested in Carolina, as was Martin Mylin, who was Mother's cousin.

Sometime after New Year's Day in 1710, the Herrs heard from people who were returning from London as to what had happened to the poor refugees from the Palatinate. Many had died while others returned to Germany. But on December 25, 1709, four thousand refugees set sail for New York in ten different ships. The people of London and the British government, frustrated and angry at the crowds of refugees, on December 30 had forbidden any further arrivals except for those who could pay their own way. That slowed the emigration down to a mere trickle.

Hans kept shaking his head. "The Quakers told us winter is the wrong time of year to sail. The winds are often not favorable and the voyage takes too long. People become sick and many die." He shook his head again. "And many of those persons were not in good health to start with," he added.

A few days later, new reports arrived from Switzerland about arrests in Bern. There was talk of shipping those arrested to America. Once again they appealed to the Dutch Mennonites for aid. The Dutch government had before brought pressure on the Swiss to treat these people less harshly. Another letter of appeal was written by Nicholas Musser of Bern, an elderly minister, who we heard later died in prison.

The Dutch Mennonite response was a meeting in Amsterdam on February 24-25, 1710. Out of this meeting, grew a new committee called "Funds for Foreign Needs." Few indeed could have foreseen how great a work this was to prove in the years ahead, in settling poverty-stricken Mennonites from Switzerland and Germany in the American colony of Pennsylvania, in an area that was later to become known as Lancaster County.

True, this committee and its funds, as well as its patience, was often strained to the breaking point. Destitute Mennonites often viewed these benevolent Dutch people as an answer to their prayers, and in the years ahead turned deaf ears to all their advice to stay where they were and receive help there.

Slowly, a small group began making plans to leave in early spring: Hans Herr, Uncle Martin Kendig, the Jacob Miller family, and the Martin Mylin family. Martin Oberholtzer wasn't sure yet.

Christian and Anna had married quietly that winter and moved in with his parents. They discussed the move once more.

"I want to do what you think best," agreed Anna, "but I would feel so much better if a minister would go along. Like your parents. Otherwise we would be like sheep without a shepherd."

Christian nodded. "Let's ask them," he said.

Neither Father nor Mother said much when Christian asked them the next morning. But Father sent Isaac to tell Hans and Abraham to come that evening.

"Well, what do you say?" asked Father. "Shall we all go?"

Abraham took a deep breath. "Why don't you all go? Anna and I were thinking of going, but we've heard the voyage is hard for children. Maybe in a few years, when our children are older, we'll come too. And it seems Isaac and Emanuel aren't too keen on going, because all their friends are here. They could live with us and continue farming your fields for now. And we could work together in harvest."

Father looked at Isaac and Emanuel and they nodded at him. "That way we'd still have the land, and we and Abraham could help each other," Isaac said.

"We'll need to pray about this some more," said Father, as Mother nodded her head. "My parents thought they moved far away when they came from Switzerland and that was 150 miles. This would be the other side of the world."

The next morning Mother said, "We are too old to go."

"You're both still hard-working," answered Christian.

"But we don't want to start all over in a new land. We're too old for that," objected Mother.

"You can live with us," said Christian, "and let Emanuel and Isaac take over here if they don't want to go along."

Hans and Martin Kendig came the next evening to visit Father and Mother. Before the men left, they had Father's promise that if they could not find a younger minister to go with them, they would be willing to go. Father's parting words to them were, "Don't forget as you plan, if we live, and the Lord wills." Soon the men were gone into the night.

Mother commented, "Years ago, when we left Switzerland at the invitation of the Elector Count Karl Ludwig, we never dreamed that the Palatinate would someday seem so much like home. Why, none of the children talk like the Swiss anymore, but instead speak the dialect of the local people here." Yet sometimes she had heard others complain, "Here we are, working day in and day out as hard as we can so the rich can live in ease on our taxes and be clothed in silks and velvets." And what was it that Christian had said? "Where will we find places for our children? We are already overcrowded here and the local people are trying to get our farms. New taxes could be added at any time." It was hard to know what to think.

*   *   *

After much discussion, the Herrs decided to go to Carolina. Plans were made to leave by the middle of March. Soon more people were interested in the venture. The list of people planning to go soon grew to twenty-nine. Besides Father and Mother, Hans and Christian, there were the Martin Oberholtzers, Martin Kendigs, Jacob Millers, and Martin Mylins. Bread was baked, cut up, and baked again so it would not spoil. Kitchen tools, knives, and small tools were packed in small wooden barrels or chests along with any extra clothes. The men met to decide what tools to take and what tools to sell. It was interesting to see wooden handles removed to make packing of tools easier.

The whole group would only take one large chest with each family taking several smaller chests and small barrels. Into the larger chest would go the larger tools and Hans' big *Froschauer* Bible. Many of the families did not have a complete Bible, but most had their New Testaments, and the *Ausbund,* the song book they used. The women's

spinning wheels were taken apart and the most complicated parts placed
into the chests. Anna made a small bag to tie to her waist. In it was
some linen thread and cloth, a lump of beeswax, some needles, and a
small scissors in case she needed to do some mending on the way to
America. Any possessions not needed for the journey were sold to raise
money for the ocean voyage. Friends donated hard Swiss cheeses for
the journey. Also, precious little bags of seeds were sewn and packed
in corners of the little chests.

Father and Mother went to live with Abraham and Anna for the
last few days. They tried to spend extra time with each grandchild.
Six-year-old Barbara clung to Mother. Mommy Herr had always been
so special to her. "Mommy, I wish I were going too," sobbed Barbara.

Mommy Herr held the little girl close. She did not tell Barbara
part of the reason why they weren't going. Abraham had made some
inquiries and learned that many children under six years of age did
not survive the long voyage. "Perhaps once you are older, once little
Elizabeth and baby Samuel grow up a little more. You must be Mother's
good little helper and say your prayers and learn your Bible verses
and sing the songs until I see you again."

The day before the Herrs were ready to leave, a neighbor brought
a message. In Bern, Switzerland, the official decree to ship the troublesome *Taufer* to Carolina was enforced. The Mennonite network of
contacts along the Rhine was alerted. Among themselves, the prisoners in Bern vowed to not become separated from their families by three
thousand miles of ocean. Plans were made for other Brethren to free
them when they reached Mannheim. Hearing that the main leaders,
including Benedict Brechbühl, were to be put in iron chains for the trip
down the Rhine brought fresh alarm.

Everyone shook their heads at this news. "In iron chains, to be
sent without their families. Oh God, be merciful," murmured Father.

The officials were taking no chances, knowing how often
escapes had occurred before. On March 18, fifty-seven prisoners,
including twelve women, were put on a river vessel. "We can't
imagine," said the neighbor, "the prayers, the heartaches, and the
fears, of those on the vessel as well as the loved ones they left
behind."

The Herrs had a worship service together the evening before they
left. Hans prayed for the Swiss Brethren. There were no dry eyes among
the group gathered that night. Hans spoke calmly as he committed the

Swiss to the care of a mighty God. "The same sun and moon and stars will shine for us there if it be the Lord's will that we reach that land. God surveyed all He had made and called it good. If we shall not meet again here, may we meet in that happy land where no more pain or tears shall be known. No matter where we are or what we face, God's ear can hear. He can bring comfort to our hearts." Soon peace and calm took the place of the tears.

Winter was still in the air that cold March day when the group boarded the small boat that would take them down the Rhine River. As they floated down the Rhine past cities, towns, and villages, and castles or castle ruins, there were dark evergreen forests and vineyards on hillsides, and Christian had to wonder how all this lovely scenery might look in the summertime. In some of those forests, the Brethren had hidden during the worst parts of the Thirty Years War. Almost every town collected a tax to let them pass down the Rhine. The amount was higher than they expected.

Near the town of Koblenz, the Mosel and Lahn Rivers added their waters to the Rhine. On they went, day after day, until they reached Bonn and then the city of Cologne as the river grew ever wider and more majestic. They passed Dusseldorf, and at last arrived at Wesel where the Rhine branches. On April 10, 1710, they arrived in Rotterdam.

It did not take long for the group to find Mennonites who took them in. They were much surprised at the grand houses and observed the extreme contrast of their own simple, rough homespun clothes were compared to the more fashionable Dutch clothing. But they were given food and beds. People welcomed them and told them of an aid committee in Amsterdam headed by Jan van Gent and Hendrick van Toren.

On April 13, the Dutch men wrote to the "Foreign Relief" committee and told them of the group of twenty-nine Palatine Mennonites bound for Carolina. "They plan to sail on their own, without government help. They have admitted that it cost more to come down the Rhine than was expected, and they are 200 guilders short of the fare and have asked to borrow this amount from us. Perhaps you can help them," they wrote.

In the meantime, Hendrick van Toren suggested they go to Pennsylvania instead of Carolina. He told them that some of the Dutch Mennonites had been living there for twenty-five years already and that William Penn had given religious freedom and more liberty than most of the other colonies. Penn also made treaties with the Indians and bought land from them. Plus there were already Germans as well as some Swiss Mennonites at Germantown. And since 1703, there was also a settlement at Skippack. This news was discussed and inquiries from other sources were made, and the group decided to go to Pennsylvania instead, because of Penn's treaties with the Indians and more religious liberty.

Then came the return letter from the "Foreign Relief" committee at Amsterdam. They replied that although they cannot fulfill every request that they receive, since this amount was not that large, and since the group could not sail without it, they would provide what they needed. They were put under the care of Jan van Gent and Hendrick van Toren.

Since the group's arrival, they had asked about the Swiss Brethren. They were told they had also arrived, but had gotten few details. Hendrick van Toren said he would check into the matter, and on Sunday afternoon they all gathered to hear his story. Hendrick could speak some German and he told the group that the Lord had provided. There was a quiet hush; Hendrick cleared his throat.

There were some by the names of Eshelman, Brechbühl, Gerber, Graybill, Rohrer, Rupp, Shenk, Steiner, and Wenger on the boat, he told them. George Ritter was in charge and kept a tight check on all his prisoners, knowing he would be paid only for those who shipped out at Rotterdam. Already in Basel one woman had managed to slip away. But Swiss authorities had not reckoned on the indignation of alerted Dutch Mennonites who were horrified that these Swiss Mennonites, whose only crime was their faith and the way they chose to live it, should be treated as the greatest of criminals. Nor had they reckoned on the sympathy of Dutch officials, who told the Swiss ambassador that in Holland the Mennonites had always shown themselves "good inhabitants and good subjects."

Hendrick went on.

When the vessel reached Mannheim, someone persuaded Ritter to let the women, the elderly, and the sick get off. They were welcomed and cared for by the Brethren, who also sent a message ahead to the Brethren at Neuvied to look out for the twenty-two male prisoners still on board and to send word on to the Dutch Mennonites. Swiss agent Michel at this time came from England and, hearing how opposed the Dutch were to the plan, hurried up the Rhine to meet Ritter; together they tried to persuade their chained prisoners to go to America of their own free will. But even though these prisoners were chained in body, Ritter and Michel soon found out that they were not chained in spirit.

Everyone grinned as Hendrick chuckled over this part of the story.

Back in Amsterdam, the Swiss ambassador looked up the British ambassador, telling him what good farmers these people were, without mentioning why they were so anxious to be rid of them. But some of the Dutch Mennonites were experienced business-men and were not tricked by smooth talking diplo-mats. They requested that a sharp lookout be kept at all possible points along the Rhine where they might land. As the prisoners' boat floated nearer to the Dutch border, the excitement rose higher and higher. At Neuvied, Mennonite Preacher Thielmann Rupp saw it coming and walked along the shore, talking to the prisoners until the guards put a stop to it.

On April 6, nineteen days after leaving, the ship entered Dutch territory at Nyjmegen. Ritter granted the request that one prisoner be allowed to visit the Mennonites there. Two guards went along to the home of Preacher Lawrence Hendricks. Hendricks could hardly understand the dialect, but gathered several other Mennonite leaders and went back to the boat. Here they persuaded Ritter to take the rest of the pris-oners along for refreshment. As they walked along, the leaders told the prisoners, "We have you now.

If the soldiers try to get you back, we'll complain to our authorities."

They were so thankful and oh, how good it felt to finally be free from the irons after nearly three weeks on the damp boat. One Dutch Mennonite wrote that they were quite a rugged folk by nature who could endure hardship. They were very zealous to serve God with prayer and Bible reading and were very simple in all their behaviors, as lambs and doves. One preached to the Mennonites at Cleves, and they were received there as heroes. They had lived so long on bread and water that they could not tolerate eating meat and even turned down an offer of beds, preferring straw.

They parted with them with tearful embraces. Brechbühl and the rest started back on foot, heading for Mannheim where some of the wives had been left off.

In Amsterdam, it was like a kettle of boiling stew. The Swiss ambassador, meeting with the British ambassador, found the conference room full and overflowing with Dutch Mennonites from nearly every Dutch province. Everyone was excited to a fevered pitch. They had already appealed to the British ambassador for Queen Anne's help. Almost overwhelmed, the Swiss ambassador tried to explain his government's position on the prisoners. They refused to go to war, and if they were expelled to the borders, they kept returning. If they would cooperate and go to America, they could have their freedom and be able to support themselves.

Finally, a compromise was reached. The Dutch Mennonites would go to Nyjmegen and get the prisoners to promise not to go back to Bern. But by the time the Mennonites reached Nyjmegen, the prisoners were already well on their way to Mannheim. When they caught up with the prisoners, the Mennonites requested that Brechbühl, whose family was still in Switzerland, return with the other leaders to Amsterdam.

> *Two weeks later, Brechbühl and four other lead-*
> *ers were in Amsterdam, telling their story to Menno-*
> *nite leaders and city officials. They compared their*
> *lot with those characters of the Dutch "Martyrs Mir-*
> *ror" and explained why they were unwilling to leave*
> *their homeland.*

As Hendrick finished his narrative, the group sighed with relief. How good it was to know that their Brethren had escaped harm. They were so glad for the intervention of the Dutch Mennonites on their behalf.

Thus, on April 23, less than two weeks after their arrival at Rotterdam, the Palatine Mennonites boarded a ship for London. They said their good-byes to the helpful Dutch Mennonites and slowly went down the fourteen-mile-long canal to the open sea. Now they were dependent upon the winds. *Oh Lord, we are in Thy hands,* thought Christian as he remembered what his brother Hans had told him. It would take anywhere from eight days, with favorable winds, to four weeks to sail from Rotterdam to England. As they came into the North Sea and out into the Strait of Dover, they held their breath in awe as they gazed at the magnificent rocky White Cliffs of Dover rising for more than one hundred feet above the coast of Kent.

Christian Herr's ship took about two weeks, but it was long enough to get a taste of ship life and learn what crowded quarters were like below decks.

Arriving in London, the Herrs checked around for ships leaving for Pennsylvania. Although one had left not long ago and they had missed it, there were none at present. Now they would have to wait. How long, no one knew. Christian thought back to his talk with Mother when he'd said, "It's this not knowing that's so hard." He thought of the Swiss Brethren and of how God had provided for them. Slowly a peace flowed into his heart. Hans was already meeting with Quakers he'd learned to know last year. Last year's burdens were already helping this year's problems. Yes, God was good.

CHAPTER FOUR

The Herr family went to an inn to sleep for the night. The next day the women and children waited at the inn while the men went to see what they could accomplish.

By evening, Hans returned and told of having found some Quakers he'd met last year who had provided some helpful advice. Since it might be a month or even longer before they could expect to sail, the men would try to find work in exchange for board so they wouldn't all have to stay at the inn. That way they would not have to use money needed for passage on the ship. Father and Martin Kendig would make a daily journey to the docks to see about a ship.

The women made arrangements for the washing of clothes. Early on Sunday the Mennonites gathered together under some trees for a quiet worship service. They did not sing, as they did not want to attract attention.

A few of the men then went with their Quaker friends to their worship services. Little walks were taken in the afternoon and evening as they explored the neighborhood where they were staying. Everything was fresh and green and growing. It made them a bit homesick as each thought of what the trees and fields at home might look like.

On Monday, Father and Martin Kendig came with the exciting news that a ship had docked from Pennsylvania. Tomorrow all available men would go to the docks to talk with the captain. Perhaps they could soon be on their way. It was an anxious day for all. Anna, Frances, and Mother eagerly waited for news. It was late when the men returned.

"What took so long?" asked Mother.

"Oh, they were unloading the ship and the captain was busy. They had furs and lumber and flaxseed and other things they were unloading, but mostly furs. The ship is called the *Mary Hope* and is a small, unarmed ship. The captain is John Annis. We may have to wait another three weeks or more before she sails. They want to make a few repairs, and they will wait to sail with several other ships. They say there is considerable danger from the French fleet, as well as from pirates."

Christian bowed his head. The war that had made life hard and troublesome for them in the Palatinate was even reaching its fingers into their life here. America was so far away. Would it be far enough away that the wars here would not touch their lives there? Was it possible they would follow them over the ocean too? Was their venture to be plagued by the troubles and trials experienced by William Penn? Was trouble always behind him like a dog following at a distance, ever waiting for a chance to nip at his heels?

Hans sighed. "The Quakers say it would be a good idea to take some extra food along on our own. If the ship becomes crowded, the food will not reach; or it may spoil if the voyage takes longer than we expect."

"Maybe we could get more food from the Quaker farmer you worked for last summer, Hans," Father pondered.

"I don't see how we could get enough to make much difference for twenty-nine people, but perhaps the Friends will help with what we need. I heard they gave money to the group that went to Germantown last year, but, of course, they can't help every group. The Friends are already doing a lot for us," said Hans.

"Very well," said Father. "Oh, there is some good news. The captain expects to sail on June 6."

"At last," said Mother, "that is good news."

The next evening it was nearly dark when Martin Kendig stopped by with a Quaker man, who could speak some German. Each person introduced himself.

"Now that you are here," said Father to the Quaker, "I'd like to inquire about the many Palatines who were here the last two years. The numbers we've heard are almost unbelievable. Yet Hans, here, saw them last summer and he says he believes them. What is your opinion?"

"Well, they say that in the two years of 1708 and 1709 there were as many as 13,000 people who came from Germany because they heard that Queen Anne would send them to America at her expense. Many were families who suffered in the war with Catholic France. They probably would have put a stop to this sooner, except that our government was of the opinion that more people for America would mean more wealth for England. But London was just not prepared to feed so many people for so long. Lack of food and the crowded conditions brought all kinds of diseases. Far, far too many of them died here. Some say about one-third."

The Quaker shook his head as he continued. "Some were sent to Ireland, and about 4,000 were sent to New York on December 25. They were to make tar and turpentine for the British navy to pay for their passage."

The man shook his head again. "These people needed to build homes and clear land. I keep wondering how the trip went . . . in winter . . . across the Atlantic . . . when the winds often blow the wrong way. I wonder if the ones who were best off were not the 7,000 or so who returned home again."

"Yes," agreed Hans. "While some died and many suffered in the war with France, good Queen Anne felt sorry for these people. They came to her for help and in the meantime they died by the thousands, from disease and lack of food instead of from war." He shook himself as if trying to shake off the memory.

Now Martin Kendig said, "We've got some good news and some bad news. The good news is that Samuel Guldin and his wife Susanna and their three children are also going on our ship. Samuel is a Reformed minister who is also a Pietist. You know it is many of the Pietists in Switzerland who sheltered and aided the persecuted Swiss Brethren near Bern.

"He has quite the story to tell. He said he was sick and in misery for nine months after he started his ministry. But he said that on August 4, 1693, the light of faith rose within him, and he began to preach with new power, so that his sermons were different. In time this led to trouble with the council at Bern. He was called before them and asked to recant his pietism. When he refused, he was banished from Bern and from his church, which was the largest one in the city. For a time he had churches out in the country, but he was forced to flee to North Germany and now has booked passage on the *Mary Hope* and is going to Pennsylvania too. He even knows some of the persecuted Brethren at Bern.

"And now for the bad news," said Martin. "The way it looks, we will not be sailing on June 6 after all. There are several other ships which will be sailing with us. They want to meet with a convoy of Russian warships and go across the North Sea with them, as they feel there are too many French warships in the area."

Mother sighed once more. "Lord, grant us patience." It was already about seven weeks since they had arrived in London. She had been helping with the cooking and washing dishes at the inn where they were staying. Most of the rest of their group were staying with Quaker families, as an inn was a poor place to stay with small children for any length of time. But they had not expected to partake of the hospitality of the Friends for so long. This long waiting was affecting everyone.

When Hans heard the news that they would not be sailing on June 6 after all, he asked Christian, "Will you go with me to the Quaker farmer outside of London for whom I worked for last year?"

Christian nodded. "That might be a good idea."

"But what if they decide to sail while you are out there?" Frances worriedly asked.

Martin Kendig spoke up. "Why don't Marcus Oberholtzer and I go with you. We can come back the next day if you find work. Then we should be able to get word to you should the ship want to leave. And we can see what Hans' friend can do for us as far as obtaining extra food to take along. We should have some butter and cheese if we can purchase them at a decent price."

As the Mennonites approached the farm, Hans explained, "Farmer James has had a German workman for two years and knows some German words. I also learned a few English words, but we communicate mostly by sign language."

The first thing they saw was a flock of sheep grazing in a meadow surrounded by stone walls. "Those are his sheep," said Hans. "Over in the next meadow, I see three cows and a calf, but I don't see the other two cows."

Farmer James must have heard them talking. He came up to them with a very big smile. He grabbed Hans' hand and held on for awhile. At last he asked, "Frances?" and then used his hand to show three little sizes.

Hans nodded and smiled, *"Gute—Gute."* (Good, Good) Then he pointed to Christian, then to himself and said, *"Bruder—*Christian."

Farmer James made motions to show he thought they looked alike and nodded. "Brother," he said, and nodded some more.

"Martin Kendig," said Martin as he introduced himself. Then he turned to Marcus Oberholtzer and introduced him as well.

Hans drew an outline of a ship with a tall sail and said, "America . . . Penn's Woods . . . William Penn." Again there was the nodding of heads.

Hans made motions of milking cows and held up three fingers, then shrugged as if asking and held up five fingers. A sad, woebegone expression crossed the farmer's face. He made motions with his hands and head to show they had died.

"Tod . . . Tod?" asked Hans.

"Ya . . . yes," nodded James. "Dead." And he held up two fingers and shook his head. He shrugged and held up his hand to show there was nothing he could do about it.

Hans made an up-and-down motion as if churning butter and then as if he were spreading butter on a piece of bread. *"Butta?"*

"Ya . . . ya, butter." He shook his head slowly, sadly. *"Net . . . net,* no butter."

Hans made a milking motion again and a small round shape and pretended to use a knife to slice it. *"Kase?"*

"Net . . . net! No *kase . . .* no cheese." Again he held up his two fingers and showed his cows dying, showing if the cows hadn't died, then *ya, butta un kase . . .* butter and cheese.

Once more Hans showed a sailing ship and an eating motion. James nodded understandingly and showed empty palms. Then he shrugged and motioned them to come. He showed them a nice garden, with peas hanging on their stalks, lettuce, beets, carrots, and beans growing. This was all he had to give, but he drew a big sail and shook his head. *"Net gute."*

Martin Kendig nodded agreement, *"Net gute."* (Not good on a ship.)

Hans pointed to himself and Christian and their hands and said, "Work? Eat?" He pointed to the garden. He held up ten fingers, closed them, again held up five more and shrugged and again held up five more and shrugged once more as he made a large sail.

"Ya, ya, ship not sail," answered James.

Hans then took the men to the small shed where he and Frances had stayed last summer. There were tools and several barrels in there. He tried to tip one but saw it was full.

James chuckled. *"Kraut!"* He chuckled again and shook his head. "Cabbages." He motioned with a wide sweep of his arms, showing Hans that there were a lot of cabbages last year.

Hans nodded. He had helped plant and weed the cabbages and knew there were a lot of them.

"German farmer want put in *keller* (cellar) for winter and then sell," James said. Then he made motions to show rain coming down. "Rain, lots of rain." He made a round motion with his hands and then a cut or split of the round head.

There was a murmur of assent and all four men nodded their heads. Too much rain made cabbage heads split. No good.

James made cutting and slicing and pounding movements. "Saurkraut—all saurkraut. We no like." He shook his head.

Hans asked, "Where German farmer?"

"New York. December 25." He drew a big sail. *"Freundschaft* (relatives) all go." He made a motion of a smaller barrel and showed it on his shoulder and pointed down the road and then a sail again. A light seemed to flicker, as suddenly it dawned on all four men at once that here was food they could take on the ship! There was a quiet whispered conversation. Someone wondered how they would get it to the ship.

"Roll it," suggested Christian with a shrug.

Martin Kendig grumbled, "Only as a last resort. Ask him if he knows of a way to get it to the ship, or at least to London."

Hans went through all the motions. James cleared his throat several times, then said, "Neighbor Henry, Quaker" and pointed over the hill. Hans nodded. He made a motion to show big wheels—cart. Then he said, "Horse" and "London."

When there were nods all around, he held up several fingers and shrugged. He added a few more fingers and then shrugged again.

Martin Kendig held out his palm and drew a round circle, show-ing money, and that they had very little. James pointed to himself and Hans and over the hill and said, "Neighbor Henry" and then made an eating motion. Hans said, "Eat saurkraut."

Christian saw he was trying to say they would go see neighbor Henry and then they would eat. James suddenly left for the house and was soon back. They all walked over the hills and meadows to neighbor Henry's.

It took awhile, but at last it was arranged that Marcus Oberholtzer would help Henry for several days until Henry was ready to go to London and take their barrels of saurkraut along. Martin Kendig would head back to London the next morning.

That night as Christian lay in the barn on his bed of straw, he pondered the day's happening. They had hoped to buy a bit of butter and cheese at a decent price and it had been disappointing to find that there was none. Now to find several whole barrels of saurkraut was surely a Godsend! *Plain food for common plain people,* he thought.

Yes, God does provide if we are satisfied. Christian remembered how disappointed he'd been that the ship hadn't sailed yet. Somehow the burden of tension that had built up the last while seemed to fade away and trust and peace took its place once more. *Thanks be to You, Lord,* thought Christian as he fell asleep.

Marcus Oberholtzer headed for London about a week later. Hans and Christian helped James for two weeks, then they headed back to London where they were greeted with good news. The Dutch had sent the money.

At last came the news that the Mennonites would sail June 24, nearly ten weeks after they had arrived in London. What a relief to be on their way. Only God knew what lay ahead.

At the same time the *Mary Hope* was getting ready for the long voyage, another ship was also preparing to sail for Carolina. Swiss agent Michel was taking a group of people there to start a settlement called New Bern. Michel had beguiled many more people with his smooth stories of non-existent rich silver mines in Pennsylvania. Some German miners even went to work in the mines. This ship started loading on June 20. If the group anticipating boarding the *Mary Hope* had changed their plans, they would likely have been among the group of Swiss who would build their homes at New Bern in Carolina.

The Quakers who had provided work and a place to stay came to see them off. There they met the other Quakers who had come to say good-bye to Quaker missionary Thomas Chalkley. He had come to London from Philadelphia for the Quakers' yearly meeting. It had been his third trip to London.

Christian and Hans Herr, and Martin Kendig went with their Quaker hosts to speak with the other Quakers. Mother could not understand what they were saying, but she saw Hans was frowning. They were gesturing at the ship and talking, and as they came back they were in earnest conversation, glancing at the ship every now and then. Slowly everyone filed on board, families together clutching bags and parcels, and mothers and fathers holding the hands of their children as they tried to keep an eye on everyone to make sure they were all there.

Mother and Father were the last of this group to board since they had no small children. Christian looked at each child as if to impress a picture of each one in his mind. Only the Lord knew which or how many of these dear ones might find a watery grave. Only recently Christian had found out that the first time William Penn went over in 1682 on the ship *Welcome*, smallpox had broken out. Of about one hundred passengers, thirty had died of smallpox on the way to America. He shivered a bit. "Oh, God, be merciful," he prayed. "We commit them all into Thy care."

Thomas Chalkley came to make their acquaintance, with Samuel Guldin beside him. These were not the first Swiss Brethren, or Mennonites, that he had met. Chalkley had met Mennonites on former preaching trips in Europe and had written in his journal that these people are "very near to the truth" and therefore "ripe for spiritual harvesting."

He may have been one of the first who saw the Mennonites as candidates for converts, but he was surely not the last. Later he added in his journal that he had never met with more tenderness and openness in people than in those parts of the world.

Later Mother found Hans and asked him, "When you were talking with Thomas Chalkley and that group of Quakers, what were they saying that you were frowning about?"

"Oh, was I frowning? I wasn't aware of it," said Hans as he started to walk away. Mother caught at his sleeve.

"Hans," she said sternly, "you are avoiding my question."

Hans swallowed and cleared his throat as he looked into his mother's eyes. "From what we could gather, they were trying to persuade Thomas not to get on such a small and overcrowded ship," he said softly. "They put in extra bunks while they were docked here."

"And what was his answer?"

"He said he had already been too long from his wife and business, although he said he knew they meant well."

Mother and son looked for a time into each other's eyes and both were silent as Hans turned and walked away.

They went down the ladders to explore below deck. It was very small and crowded. It was shadowy with some light streaming down from one of the open hatches.

"I found out," said Martin Kendig, "that when it gives a storm they close all the hatches."

The ship was not yet sailing and the children were fascinated as they watched the crew climb up the rigging, and checked the ropes and sails. They seemed so strong and fearless. There was one especially, called Big Jim, who instead of taking one small barrel at a time, would manage to take a barrel under each brawny arm and head for the other end of the ship. Mother saw her two sons look at each other silently. They knew how heavy some of those barrels were.

In the next four days before they sailed, more people came on board, and a pile of hay was stored on deck for the milk goats that could be heard bleating in their pens. There was a squawking now and then from some of the hens. The passengers passed their time by making whatever final preparations they could for the voyage.

Including the captain and deck hands, there were ninety-four people on board. *Almost one-third of those are our party,* thought Christian as he surveyed the people on the deck. It was easy to pick out his own people because of their coarse homespun and simple clothing. Samuel Guldin, his wife Susanna, and their three children, Samuel (17), Maria (14), and Emmanuel (11), were about the only ones they could speak well with. Of course, most of the sailors could speak several languages. One of the men said, "They can swear in several languages, too."

At last, on June 24, they set sail from the Thames River. The Thames was a very busy river, alive with many ships and boats, both small and large. It was a cheerful and lovely picture. The dipping of oars and the billow of sails from the vessels made a picturesque scene for the passengers who were watching from the decks.

All of a sudden, there was more shouting and a great commotion. A few of the sails were lowered in a hurry as the cry went from one to the other. "Boy overboard!" Mother and the other women looked bewildered but soon saw that a small boat had been hit.

"A boy fell overboard from that boat," said Samuel Guldin, "and it didn't look as if he could swim. They say he went down, but with all the boats and ships around, he should come up where someone can give a helping hand."

Each minute passed by seeming like eternity. After what seemed like a very long time, someone said, "They have him now, but it looks like it's too late." The shouts back and forth soon confirmed the story. The boy had drowned. A strange silence fell over the whole deck. Even the crew raised the sail once more in silence.

"Oh, merciful God," said Mother. "He was some mother's son, here only an hour ago. As we left, I thought of all the children on board. And now already, when we saw no danger at all, a life has fled."

But scarcely an hour later, the murmur of the people could be heard once more. There was another ship near by and all of a sudden there was a terrific jolt, so rough that most people lost their footing and fell. At the same time, there was a terrible cracking and splintering of wood. Children started to cry. The *Mary Hope* had hit the other ship. The corners were knocked from her, but the other ship was damaged much more. There were angry shouts from the other ship, and one of the crew shook his fist. It was rather an unhappy start for the first day.

Three days later, a British warship came ever nearer. The ship came up beside them and gave orders for them to stop. "What does a British warship want with us?" asked Martin Kendig.

They soon found out that the captain was arrested for crashing into the other ship three days ago, and he was taken on the warship. The crew was directed to go onto Gravesend where another captain would replace him.

Once more the people fell silent for a time. "It's too bad he didn't pay attention and hit that other ship," said Christian. "He seemed like a fine man."

"Yes," nodded Samuel Guldin, " I thought so too, except for one thing. A man came to him about something, I'm not sure what; but he had a paper that John Annis had signed and he waved it at him. The captain took the paper and tore off his name, which wasn't right. But it is too bad. He seemed to know what he was doing. Maybe it's to remind us that we shouldn't put our trust in men."

"I know," answered Christian. "I was reminded of that when those Quakers tried to tell Thomas Chalkley the ship was too small and crowded."

On July 12, they reached Harwich. That morning Father came and asked Mother, "Do you and the rest of the women want to hear the letter Martin Kendig has written to send to the Friends in Amsterdam to thank them for the help we have been given?"

"Yes, I think I should like to hear it," said Mother. "I'll tell the rest of the women." Later as they assembled on deck, Martin read:

Worthy and Beloved Friends:

> *Besides wishing you all temporal and eternal welfare, we have wanted to inform you that we have received the financial aid which the dear friends out of the goodness of heart have given toward our journey. This kind contribution came very opportunely to us, because the journey cost more than we imagined. God bless the worthy friends in time and eternity: and whatever may be of good for the body and wholesome for the soul may the merciful God give them and continually be and remain their rewarder. But of our journey we report that we were detained almost ten weeks, before we were put on board ship, but then we actually entered into the ship on the 24th, were well lodged and well cared for, and we have been informed that we will set sail from here next Saturday or Sunday from Gravesend, and wait there for the Russian convoy. God be with us and bring us to land in America as happily as here in England. Herewith we commend you to the merciful God; and should we not see one another in this life, may God permit us to see one*

another in eternity. Wherewith we commend you to merciful God together with courteous greetings from us all and remain your true friends. London, the 27th of June, 1710.

Signed:

Martin Kendig
Jacob Muller
Martin Oberholtzer
Martin Mylin
Christian Herr
Hans Herr

CHAPTER FIVE

Early on July 13, the Herrs saw the Russian fleet in the distance. It was Sunday and the Quaker preacher, Thomas Chalkley, held a sermon on deck. By Sunday evening they caught up with the fleet.

"Those Russian ships kept getting bigger all day," stated one of the children. A chuckle went through the crowd and the little boy looked bewildered.

Samuel Guldin patted him on the head. "You are right that those ships are very big. In fact, they make me feel that those big ships seem like huge castles, while our small ship is only a little house. But the Lord can take care of little ships, too."

"Oh, look, look! Did you see those big fish jumping?"

Soon everyone gathered at the side of the ship, and time after time they saw fish jumping all over the ocean. One of the crew made a remark about them, and Hans asked Samuel Guldin what the man had said.

"He said those are porpoises, but the sailors call them 'storm fish.' When the 'storm fish' jump, there will soon be a great storm."

Everything was so bright and beautiful, with seagulls soaring in the distance, but sometimes they flew close to the ship. It was hard to imagine that a great storm was coming.

But the next day, the winds and rains came with such a great driving force that the passengers feared for the ships. The hatches were closed and it was dark below. Many lay below deck, seasick. Quite a few of the crew were sick, including Big Jim. The storm continued the next day, and finally when it was over on the July 17, the ships turned back toward Harwich. The tall masts on several ships had broken and had to be replaced.

Another delay, thought Christian. The passengers were moved off the ships that needed repaired. The *Mary Hope* needed only minor repairs, so during the day while the repairs were being done, the Mennonites settled themselves on one end of the deck, where they could hear the hammering and pounding from the other ships.

"You know, Father, now that we've come down the Rhine and seen so many places, I wonder about Switzerland, our ancestral homeland. You often spoke of the mountains and meadows. What was it like? What are your memories?" asked Christian.

"I believe Switzerland to be as beautiful a country as you can find anywhere. We Herrs came from Bern, but I believe all the rest of our group here came from the Zurich area."

There was a nodding of heads. "There was a lot more grazing land in Switzerland because of the mountains. I can still hear the ring of the cow bells in the mountain meadows," said Father.

"Yes," added Mother. "I remember how happy I was once I was old enough to help rake the hay on the mountain side with the long wooden rakes and how we sang as we raked. There were sweet, gentle breezes blowing, and such beautiful Alpine flowers blooming in the springtime. Because we were persecuted, we took the mountain farms that others did not want."

"What I remember most are the mountain peaks, so way up high," said Martin Mylin, "especially the Jungfrau. It was such a beautiful sight. And there was always snow on the peaks, even in the summer. I always remember that, even though I was only a boy when we had to leave."

"Yes," added Marcus Oberholtzer, "the Jungfrau was beautiful, but so were the Eiger and the Monch, too. They were all very high. Especially at sunrise and sunset they were so beautiful, I'll never forget them. All the little streams coming down the mountains with the gurgling noises they made. I'd sit beside them when I was herding cows, just to hear their music. I could hear the bumblebees and the birds too. It was so peaceful in the warm sunshine as I looked down the mountain at the houses and villages and *hofs* below, and then up to the next mountains in the distance."

"Yes, very beautiful," agreed Martin Kendig heartily. "But if we get to America, I'd rather look for good dark soil like we had in the Palatinate."

There was a murmur of agreement from both the men and women. "Yes, good land, that's what we need," agreed Father, "and God's blessings on it. We were only allowed to rent land in the Palatinate. Hopefully in Penn's Woods, or Pennsylvania as they call it, we can once again own land, Lord willing. Penn has made special offers of credit to settlers he trusts."

Christian had another question. "Father, why did the local people sometimes accuse us of using black magic with our land? Neighbor Dan once shook his fist at me when he saw how much more wheat was in our field. He said if we didn't use black magic, our fields wouldn't get better while theirs got poorer."

Father cleared his throat. "In Switzerland, we learned to make hay to feed the cattle over the winter, while others only fed their cattle straw. But in the Palatinate, we had no mountain meadows to make hay. Years ago when one of the Dutch ministers came to visit, he brought along a bag of clover and long grass seed. Some say it came from Holland, some say Belgium, I don't know. It doesn't really matter. We began using that for hay in the winter. But we soon learned that we got better crops following clover and grass. It improved the land and provided hay for the cattle, and of course, there was the dung, which we used for fertilizer. Then the next year, we'd plant the clover in another field. We learned by moving the clover and other crops around, the fields gave better crops. Neighbor Dan, who shook his fist at you, had grain in that field for as long as I can remember," said Father.

"Yes, and if they hadn't seen us as heretics and looked down on us, they might have seen what we were doing to make the land better," added Martin Kendig, "instead of blaming it on black magic."

Mother agreed, "You can't learn much from a person you look down upon," she said.

"For how long have the Anabaptists or Mennonites been called heretics?" asked Hans.

"Well, about 185 years or so. The old people used to say that Conrad Grebel baptized George Blaurock and that he and Felix Manz were martyred not long after 1525, which was soon after the Anabaptists began. For many years there were a lot who died for their faith, thousands of them."

"Yes," said Mother, "the old people used to say that most families had at least one member who was martyred."

Frances spoke up. "Grandfather used to say that the blood of the martyrs was the seed of the church."

"That's what the old people always said," stated Martin Kendig, and there was a nodding of heads.

"Yes," added Father, "once people recognized that we were people who had a faith they were willing to die for—one that really counted—they wanted to know more about it. But the martyrs . . . they still live on for us today. Many of our songs were written by men in prison like Hans Landis who would long be forgotten if it were not for the song. It is nearly one hundred years since his death. In fact, his was the last martyr's death in Zurich, I believe. But we have his song because he died a martyr's death . . . he lives on in the song, or his faith still does."

"We've got the Dursrutti song, too."

"Yes, and the Haslibacher song."

Someone started the song and they softly sang together. One song followed another until it was time for the evening meal and then back to their bunks for the night.

The next morning, Hans said, "I've been thinking a lot more about the songs we sang yesterday. Weren't a lot of our songs written by men in the dungeon of the castle at Passau? Doesn't someone know more of that story?"

"Yes," nodded several of the men, "there's more." A silence fell as they all waited for someone to begin.

"Some years before," began Father slowly, "there had been quite a number of the believers martyred at Passau. This turned the local people against the authorities and they did not wish to repeat that. So when they arrested more believers, they put them in the dungeon, or cellar, some might say, of a fortress or castle called the Oberhaus Castle, high on the hill in a place where three rivers met at Passau. The Danube and the Inn Rivers both start near the Alp Mountains of Switzerland, as does the Rhine we came down on, but the other two rivers end up in the Black Sea. The Ilz River also joins the other two rivers at Passau. Some call Passau the City of Three Rivers. But there the believers were imprisoned together for five years and a few of them were only teenagers, some of whom died from the harsh conditions.

"It was there, under the worst of conditions, that they put together these songs and sang them together with tunes of other songs they knew. And while some of their number died in the prison, we don't know for sure when these songs were first written down. Possibly not until someone wrote them down after they were released from prison. With fifty people together, singing was one of the best things they could do, both as worship and as a way to keep their faith and spirits strong. Those fifty or so hymns were the start of our song book, the *Ausbund*."

"I know that in Switzerland a lot of the persecution was because we didn't go to war," said Christian. "The Bible teaches us not to kill or use the sword and that has been an important part of our faith. But why was this seen as such a threat if we harmed no one?" asked Christian.

Martin Mylin spoke up. "Switzerland was a smaller, landlocked, mountainous country. It trained soldiers who were hired to other countries to fight for them. This was a very important source of income. They were afraid if more and more people should become unwilling to fight . . . it seemed like a great threat to the rulers. It undermined their income and power, as did also our refusal to attend the state church. They were fearful of losing their power over the people, so much so that they convinced themselves that they were doing what was right, just like the Pharisees in Jesus' time. Believer's baptism scared them too, because that would mean not everybody was a church member."

"I've often wondered," said Frances, "why people have started to call us *Menonisten* (Mennonites), when Menno Simons wasn't the one who started the Anabaptists?" *note*

Father nodded, "Menno Simons had been a Catholic priest, but he was the one who did a lot of writing about our beliefs. His writings traveled far beyond the borders of Holland. Dietrich Phillips also did some writing in Holland. And, there is also another big book, nearly as large as my Bible, that the Dutch have called the *Martyr's Mirror*. Unlike Menno Simons' writings, it has never been translated into German. It's my hope that someday it will be. It contains many stories of those martyred for their faith."

"Yes," said Martin Mylin, "my grandfather, Hans Mylin, Sr., of Zurich, was imprisoned and tortured. My father and Uncle Martin were also put in prison; and in 1639, Barbara and Elizabeth too. Uncle Martin was a historian and kept records of the persecutions from Zurich for about nineteen years, from 1639 to 1658. Those records were used in part of the *Martyr's Mirror*. I too hope that some day that book will be printed in the German language so I can read it. I looked at one while we were in Holland and it contained detailed pictures as well."

"I have to think back to last winter when it was so cold," said Hans, "when all our turnips and beets and cabbage froze in the root cellars, like they had never done before. If it hadn't been for our practice of burying some root crops outside in case the soldiers took ours, we would have had very little to eat by spring time, as the frozen things didn't keep long once they thawed. What I was wondering about was that some people talked of burying their Bibles and song books at times. What all did our people bury?"

Father chuckled. "They buried almost anything they valued and didn't want taken or destroyed. You probably don't remember it any-more, but back in 1689 when we knew there were French soldiers in the area, I buried all my iron tools. First I greased them with pig fat and I buried my broadax and my chisels. Before closing the hole, I added my shovel too. We used sharp stones to dig them out when spring came. In fact, someone once said, 'These Anabaptists won't fight for their things; they'll just bury them instead.'" The whole group chuck-led over that statement.

Three days later, on July 20, the ships were again ready to sail. On the morning of July 24, they reached New Castle where they were joined by another ship heading for Carolina.

Again a storm came up and that night there was a great jolting and a bumping. They had hit another ship again! It was an anxious night. Everyone knew that the storm might again bump them into a ship and do much damage. The next day the wind was favorable once more, and they continued on.

But just at dusk, they saw ships appearing in the distance. **Large ships! War ships!** The excitement of the crew and the tone of their voices showed that they were frightfully alarmed. Feverishly they counted the ships. There were seven of them, all flying the French flag. Fear and excitement rose to a high pitch.

Samuel Guldin spoke to some of the fearful passengers, "The Lord said to Israel through Moses. 'Do not fear, stand firm and you will see the salvation of the Lord. As you have seen the Egyptians this day, you will hence forth see them no more.' That's found in Exodus 14:13-14."

It was perhaps the most anxious night of all. Many were the prayers that rose from the crowded quarters below the deck.

Samuel Guldin wrote in his diary:

> *You could hear how the thoughts of men came to the surface, and where there was trust in God or in creatures; but of trust in the Lord, there was no evidence in many.*

Christian and Anna both felt tired and weary the next morning. Very little sleep had been had by anyone except for the children throughout the long night. They were in the hands of God as they had so often been before in times of danger. But soon a different tone could be heard, full of surprise and awe.

Christian came down from above deck where he had gone sometime before dawn. "Our prayers have been heard. There is such a heavy fog we can hardly see more than a few feet ahead. It's really almost like a pillar of smoke. We can't see any other ship and no other ship can see us! The wind is changing. We can sail westward."

It was foggy the next three days, although not as much as it had been that first morning after they had spotted the ships. But they saw the French warships no more. They did see many cliffs as they passed. Samuel Guldin pointed different landmarks out to them. "See, there to the left is Scotland and on our right are islands."

On the morning of July 30, he showed them an island called Mainland, part of the Orkneys, on their left and others on their right.

"Now look closely, that's the last land you'll see for many weeks. Once you see land again, you'll be in America." There was a clear and pleasant sky and there was a good southwesterly wind. Slowly, slowly, they watched the land fade from sight until the last speck disappeared.

There were five small ships in all. One was going to New England; one to Carolina; one to Jamaica; one to Guiana, South America; and of course, the *Mary Hope* was going to Philadelphia.

Young Hans came with the news. "The storm fish are jumping again." Everyone went to the rail to watch the porpoises. Christian couldn't help but notice that watching them wasn't quite as exciting anymore, knowing that a storm was indeed coming. The wind was brisk and soon Samuel Guldin came to tell them that the sailors had said they had made eight miles an hour that morning as they were leaving the land behind them. Soon the winds got stronger and the skies darkened. They could tell they were going faster. Christian could see that the captain was becoming alarmed and he soon gave the order for the large top sails to be taken down.

Christian saw the storm approaching and asked Samuel Guldin, "How does your family do it? Not one of you was seasick in the other storm."

"We don't eat any of the salt meat. It's too salty to start with and then they also cook it in salt water. I'm convinced it's not healthy," he said.

Christian said, "We could start eating our sauerkraut with our bread we soak in water. Ship's fare is the worst part of sailing, some say. It's unhealthy and unpalatable."

As the winds increased, the ship continued to travel fast with only the lower sails. The next day, which was the first of August, while the large top sails were down, someone spread the alarm about noon.

"A ship! A ship! It might be pirates!"

The other ships were armed and prepared to fight, but as the *Mary Hope* was unarmed, the captain gave the orders to prepare to flee at short notice. "We'll take the chance of full sail even in this wind, should the ships be dangerous."

But soon they saw it was not a pirate ship and no one intended any harm. They waved as they passed in the distance, and everyone calmed down again. Toward evening the wind changed to the south-east, but the stormy weather was not yet over.

On the third of August, there was a great shout. "Whales! Whales! Oooh! See!" The surprise and awe changed to stunned silence as the whales blew water high, high into the air. The size of them was un-believable.

"You know," said Father, "that is one of God's great wonders I never expected to see. All these past few weeks, I've been wondering at the vastness of the ocean and the Great God who made them so. But I suppose the whales in the ocean are no bigger, in comparison to the vastness of the ocean, than were the fish we used to catch in the streams in Switzerland when I was a boy."

"Mother," said Hans, "a few of the men have suggested that tonight after the small children are asleep, we all come on deck to watch the stars and have a short service."

"That sounds like a good idea," answered Mother.

That night, one by one the Mennonites climbed up to the deck and stood in awed silence. The stars seemed so much closer and brighter. A solemn hush fell over them, then softly some started to sing, "*Herr Gott, Thu mich erhoren, Elend und arm bin ich, Neig Su mich dine ohren, Bewar mich seel bitt ich Hilf Herr dem dienen knecht. Dann ich thu mich ferlassen. Ganzlich auf deine reicht.*"

Hans spoke of God's love and care and the need to trust Him. Then he had a prayer and silently they went to bed.

Now that they had seen whales once, they were on the lookout for more. The next day they saw none. On August 5, there was a perfect calm, with no wind at all. The sails hung limp and it seemed strangely quiet without the creaking of the ship and the flapping of the sails.

Eleven-year-old Emmanuel Guldin came to tell them this news. "One of the sailors told my father that on one trip they were becalmed for two whole weeks! Two whole weeks," he said again.

Hardly anyone was aware that the "calm" was over until the sails began to fill up and flap a bit. A wind was coming out of the southwest. The next day, once more the cry of "Whales! Whales!" was heard. The passengers watched in silence until once more the whales threw water high up into the air.

The wind continued in the same direction on August 8-9 and during that time the ships that were heading for Jamaica and Guiana turned southward. The Mennonites watched them until they passed from sight. Now there were only three ships left.

Later, as the Herrs were talking things over, Hans asked, "How are the sick ones?"

"Better, for the most part, I'd say," answered Mother. "Thank God. But Big Jim is still sick. I told Samuel Guldin that he could take him some sauerkraut juice, but when he went over to the crew's quarters and offered him some, Big Jim refused it. He was rather sick then, and Marcus tried to nurse him a bit. But later he got even worse and sent one of the other crew members to ask for some juice. It seemed to make him feel better, but Marcus was so alarmed that he went to the captain and asked for some wine for him. Big Jim couldn't understand why he and some of the others were sick, and here Samuel Guldin's children are all healthy, and our little children are too. Perhaps that is one of the advantages of a little ship," continued Mother. "Our men are helping the crew because some are too sick to do their work. God be praised, we are well. Did you know that Thomas Chalkley has asked to hold a service for us and have someone interpret?"

"No, I didn't know that," said Hans.

"When he was in America before, he went to the Indians and asked to hold services for them. They had a council to see if this would be permitted. When an elderly woman talked, Chalkley saw that everyone listened to her with respect, so he asked his interpreter why she was speaking and was told, 'We have found some women wiser than some men.' Her name is Conquegas and she was a queen among them. The interpreter said for many years no major decisions were made without her counsel. It turned out that her advice was to listen to Chalkley. She told them that three days earlier she had dreamed she was in London and people were listening to a preacher named William Penn. Penn told her he would soon come to the Indians and preach to them as well.

"Chalkley was then allowed to preach to the Indians. That was four years ago, but Guldin says that where the Indians lived was some of the finest land he has seen in his travels in America. The trees were thick and tall and there were lots of streams. It sounds like our own Emmental Valley in Switzerland," ended Mother.

"Yes," nodded Christian, "and like the Palatinate, too. I'll talk to the rest of the men about the services. I think I'll get Samuel to ask Thomas more about that land. Martin Kendig has been saying we don't have to settle at Germantown or at Skippack. And we have to think of the others who need a place to go. With all the trouble at Bern, I wish Benedict Brechbühl and his people would come over too."

Mother sighed, "Yes, I know, but you know that Benedict will never leave his flock. He won't leave of his own free will unless everyone comes too."

"Yes, and I'm afraid the attitude of some of them is, 'I was born in Switzerland and I'll die in Switzerland, even if it has to be in prison,'" stated Hans.

On Sunday, the men assembled on deck and listened as Thomas Chalkley's sermon was translated for them. Later, Chalkley wrote in his journal:

> *My hearers seemed tender and moved by my words. They behaved soberly and were well satisfied and I can truly say I was well satisfied also.*

On August 14, the passengers watched as the last ship accompanying them turned toward New England.

Early in the morning of August 16, once more they saw the storm fish. There was already a brisk wind that soon became stronger. As the wind became stronger, once again the large top sails were lowered. All through the night the storm continued, and on August 17, even the lower sails had to be lowered until only half a sail was kept up. The passengers were now well seasoned sailors and most of the people stayed on deck and watched the storm in all its might. The waves rose higher and higher until many feared for the ship. The ship would rise up with a wave, then shortly would drop down.

"Those waves look as high as mountains," someone remarked.

That night the rudder of the ship had to be tied fast and the ship was at the mercy of the wind and the waves. In the morning, the storm broke with a strong west wind and once more the sails were raised. After that it sailed at a good speed, covering eight miles in an hour. This wind continued for the next two days, but then once more the ship was becalmed and the sails hung limp, empty, and useless.

When the sailors started fishing and several dolphins were caught, excitement grew among the passengers. These were soon cleaned and fresh fish was served that day. Oh, what a treat after eating the same ship's fare for so many weeks. The calm lasted several days and more fishing was done.

On September 2, the people saw "flying fish," fish that jumped high into the air. Later that day theyagain saw whales in the distance. Many were following one another in imposing order and succession. Soon a wind came up and once more the ship was making a good speed of five miles an hour.

Seeing more whales another day, Samuel Guldin remarked, "They remind me of a row of cows coming down from the meadows." The other farmers agreed.

From September 10 to 12, the winds blew the wrong way. The sails had to be changed frequently to change course. This was called tacking and was like sailing in a zig-zag pattern. On September 12, the last and best wind they had had so far, provided the fastest sailing yet — nine miles an hour. For the next four days the wind continued and on the evening of September 15, as they let down the weighted line to test the depth, they touched bottom with the line. A great cry went up from the crew. The water was fifteen fathoms deep, which was the same as thirty English yards or forty-five German yards.

On the morning of September 16, land was sighted. At last the Mennonites had safely arrived in America.

CHAPTER SIX

Land! Land! How beautiful it looked to ocean-weary travelers. There was great rejoicing and thanksgiving. On that same day, they entered the mighty Delaware Bay and River so far that at long last they knew they were safe from pirates. As night arrived and they again checked the depth of the water and found it to be only six fathoms deep, they had to stop. On the morning of September 17, they waited until noon to leave, hoping to have more water with the tide of the ocean. They did not proceed very far until there was a sudden jolt and the ship abruptly stopped.

"Sand bank! We're stuck on a sand bank!"

All afternoon the crew tried to get the ship off the sand bank, and at long last they succeeded. But they had to stay at that spot for the night.

The next day they secured the services of a river pilot, and a very thoughtful one at that. "This must not be the first ship he's met this way," said Hans, seeing rejoicing everywhere as two bags of apples and peaches came aboard the ship from the other boat.

"Oh, what wonderful peaches and apples! I never saw such big ones!" exclaimed some. But others couldn't answer because their mouths were too full.

After the apples and peaches were eaten, the Mennonites were all in agreement that none had ever tasted so good before. Then Martin Mylin spoke up, "It must be a fertile and well-watered land that produces fruit such as this." There was a nodding of heads and a *"Ya, ya. Gott sei dank"* (God be thanked), and an air of thanksgiving and rejoicing as the ship continue to sail up the Delaware Bay and River.

Soon Samuel Guldin said to Hans, "Do you remember those Quakers in London who warned Thomas Chalkley not to sail on the *Mary Hope* because she was so small and crowded?" Hans nodded and Samuel continued, "Thomas says that this has been the healthiest ship he had ever traveled on. No one died on the way over, which is very, very unusual, and the water did not spoil. I believe he said this was his fourth voyage."

While they were talking, the men saw other ships coming down the Delaware, heading for the ocean.

On September 20, the *Mary Hope* arrived at New Castle on the Delaware, a part of the Penn grant. Here some of the party went ashore for the first time. They were welcomed and given food and drink, and also all the apples and peaches they could carry for those remaining on the ship.

Christian and Anna listened to the men talk as they each ate an apple. Like a cup of cold water to a thirsty soul, so was this hospitality from complete strangers.

The next day, others came on the ship and invited the captain and all the people to a dinner. The captain allowed some who had not yet been ashore to leave. Others came once again with large sacks of apples to divide among those on board.

On September 22, several of the men, including Hans Herr, Christian Herr, and Samuel Guldin, left the ship to walk towards Philadelphia following the shoreline. The next morning as dawn was breaking, they saw the city of Philadelphia in the distance. They were at the docks when the *Mary Hope* arrived at noon. At long last their journey to America was at an end, after three months and four days.

The passengers had to stay on the ship until the next day so the ship could be inspected by the customs officials. As they waited, they watched the loading and unloading of all the other ships in port. It was already a busy port and they found it almost impossible to believe that less than fifty years ago this had all been a wilderness.

Thomas Chalkley sent word to the Dutch Mennonites in Germantown to send wagons for them and their baggage while he took some of the men to the land office and Penn's agent.

It was hard for the Herrs to say good-bye to the Samuel Guldin family. They had shared so much together. The Guldins would be going to friends of their relatives until they found a house near the city.

As Mother Herr, Frances, Anna, and the children climbed on the wagon for the six-mile ride to Germantown, they waved good-bye to Thomas Chalkley, who had come to see them off. Some of the men would be walking. They marveled at the size of the city as they rode through it.

"It seems so strange for the city to have no walls," said Hans. "In Europe most of the cities still have walls."

Martin Kolb, who had come to meet them, turned and said, "Yes, it's remarkable. There is always a lot of building going on. They say Philadelphia now has at least 5,000 people. I live at Skippack and had brought a load of wheat in and I'll go back through Germantown."

"The streets are well-laid out," observed Hans.

"Yes, that was William Penn's idea to lay out the streets like a checkerboard and to make them wide. Many of the streets are named after trees, such as Walnut, Chestnut, Pine, Spruce, and Elm."

Suddenly, little Hans exclaimed in surprise, "That man is **black**!"

"Sh-hh," said Frances.

"Yes," said Martin. "He is a slave. He comes from the far away land of Africa where people are black."

"About how big is Germantown?" asked Christian.

"Oh, that's a little hard to guess. It keeps increasing all the time, but I'd guess at least two or three hundred people. Spinning flax and linen weaving are the main industries, along with paper making. Some tanning is also done. William Rittenhouse was the first Mennonite minister and also the first paper maker in America. He died two years ago, just before he was to be made a bishop or elder. Then Jacob

Gottschalk took his place as elder. We had the first baptism of eleven members and also the first communion at that time. They also built a log meetinghouse two years ago."

"Do you worship with the Dutch Mennonites then?" asked Hans.

"Yes, we do now. The first year, those of us with Swiss and German background met together by ourselves. But last year we started worshiping together. They then chose three deacons and two ministers from our group." He paused and sighed. "I was one of those chosen as minister."

"God bless you," said Father. "I, too, am a minister. I thought we were too old to make such a journey, but our two children and the rest of the group did not want to come without a minister. Is that Germantown up ahead?"

"Germantown is what they call it," answered Martin Kolb. " At one time, some called it *ArmenStettle* (Poortown), because everyone was so poor at first. I've got two brothers, Jacob and Johann, who came when I did. Christopher Zimmerman, who is bringing the other wagon, lives here too. We will try to place you with the German-speaking people as much as possible.We'll take you to Johann Anton Weber, and you can stay there for a day or so. Claus Rittenhouse and his wife can also speak German rather well since they have had German indentured help in their home and the paper mill."

As Anna Herr stepped from the wagon, her knees were unsteady. She was more tired and weak than she had realized. Soon it was all planned for them. After a short stay here, she and Christian, along with Father and Mother, would go to the Rittenhouse place outside Germantown.

Two days later, Christian and Anna were once more in a wagon heading for the Rittenhouse homestead. Anton's wife had come to say good-bye and had brought a piece of ticking to fill with straw to make a bed mattress. It was a very useful gift.

Anna's eyes gazed again on the beautiful colored trees that grew in such abundance. She took a deep breath as she saw the two stone houses. A very small one was on the high bank beside a clear, fast-flowing stream. The other, a larger house with a full upper story and attic, had a pent roof in the front which overhung over a porch made of large, flat stones. A woman came out of the larger house and her face lit up as she came to greet Mother and Anna with a kiss of welcome.

She smiled and said, "I'm Wilhelmina Rittenhouse."

A few geese squawked from the enclosed fence beside the garden. It really was beautiful and peaceful. Sheep inside a fence kept the grass around the house closely cropped, and everything had a neat, well-cared-for appearance, from the well-placed flat stone walkways to neatly shingled roofs and brick chimneys. The sun filtered through the trees beside the creek, which as it gurgled and swirled over the stones, gave a lift to the spirits. A wooden foot bridge completed the picture. How restful and peaceful.

When at last Anna found her voice, she asked, "What is the name of this creek?"

"The Indians called it the Monoshone, but most people now call it Paper Mill Run because of the paper mill. It's a branch of the Wissahickon. The Wissahickon name comes from an Indian name that sounds much the same and means Cat Fish Stream. But come inside, you must be tired. Then later we'll go to the Doddyhouse where you will sleep."

"Yes, I am tired," said Anna. "I can't understand why I tire so easily."

Wilhelmina chuckled, "If you are like I was after our voyage, it will take you at least another two weeks or more to get back on your feet. When we came over, there were some so weak they had to crawl off the ship. Some even had to be carried. But it's surprising what good food and plenty of rest will do."

"Yes, I don't believe apples and peaches ever tasted as good as those that were brought on the ship. And the fresh bread with butter and milk was perfect at the Weber's. The meat was wonderful too. They called them Indian hens, and they shoot them in the woods. Anton Weber sent his son out to hunt one just for us so he could show us what they looked like. They had red heads and long red wattles, or a sort of red beard."

Wilhelmina laughed, "I know. I remember how strange they and their gobbling were to me too at one time. They were more plentiful when we first came here. You could often hear them gobble near our house the first year when we were building. Mommy said ours was only the second house in these parts. We did not want to live in Germantown because Doddy had to be near the water to make his paper. But the other house belonged to a Swedish family. When they first arrived, they made a cave house like the first settlers did at Philadelphia. They dug holes in the banks of the Delaware, and then put saplings on for a roof covering them with bark and sod. I've heard some people call them smoky houses because most of them had no real chimneys.

"Not far from here along the banks of the Wissahickon Creek lived a group of hermits with leader Johan Kelpius. They wanted to take all the good points of the many groups, including the Mennonites, and live a more perfect Christian life. He lived in a sort of cave along the Wissahickon, spending his last days mostly alone, meditating on the second coming of Christ which he expected to be real soon. He passed away about two years ago, at the age of thirty-five."

As Mother went into the house, she smiled when she saw the large fireplace the full width of the house. It had an enormous beam and a bake oven was located in the back.

"Mommy and Doddy Rittenhouse lived here and we still use the bake oven. This is Maria," said Wilhelmina, pointing to a young girl who was using a long-handled paddle to take good smelling pies from the oven. "She has been with us for four years and has one more year before she will start out on her own."

Mother and Anna inhaled deeply. "What kind of pies are those?" Mother asked.

Wilhelmina chuckled, "That is another thing we got from the Indians. Some people call them squash or even pumpkins. We make them with molasses from the West Indies and flour and some spices if we have some. After we eat, we"ll go out to our field of maize, or some people call it Indian corn. That's also something new. And in the garden, we have a yellow root vegetable that grows vines and has a very good taste. Some people call them sweet potatoes. Maybe we can have some of those tomorrow. We got those from the Indians too, as well as different kinds of beans."

Later as Anna took her knife and cut into her piece of golden orange pie, she asked, "How is the squash prepared?"

"Oh, you peel them and cut them in pieces and cook them until they are soft, then you mash them, add the molasses, some flour, and spice if you have it."

Anna savored the taste in her mouth. M-m-m. It was good. "May we have some seed?" asked Anna.

"Why, yes, of course," answered Wilhelmina.

Claus said, "We usually only have meetings every two weeks, but since all of you came they plan to have a meeting on Sunday."

By Sunday, Mother and Father both felt strong enough to walk to meeting. "It seems about all I've done is sit outside in the sun while we prepare the apples for drying, and eat. Maybe now that Hans has my spinning wheel together and ready for work, I can soon spin again. But I'm so eager to see the others at meeting, too."

"Yes, so am I," said Father. "Claus said that on Monday morning some of our men, plus some from Germantown, are starting out to search for land up near the Susquehanna River. They were not satisfied with what they saw at Skippack. Martin Kendig, Christian, and Hans said they wanted to look elsewhere."

*   *   *

As they walked the path towards home, Mother said, "It was so good to gather with others again, to sing and listen and pray."

"How much of Jacob Gottschalk's sermon could you understand?" asked Claus.

"Oh, quite a bit more than I would have a year ago, now that we spent some time in Holland," answered Father. "I find it much easier to understand than the English, although Christian and young Hans picked up quite a bit on the way over."

After dinner at the big house with Claus, Wilhelmina, and their children, Father asked more questions about the early settlers of Germantown: the Dutch, Germans, Quakers, and Mennonites.

"Well," began Claus, "it's an intertwined story between Quaker and Mennonite as well as between those from Holland and Germany. A merchant of Amsterdam, Jacob Telner, was a Mennonite who had joined the Quakers but still called the Mennonites 'Brethren.' About 1676, he came to America to visit Quakers in New York and New Jersey. Then he returned to Krefeld, Germany, as Penn's land agent and promoted immigration to Pennsylvania. He and two others each bought 5,000 acres north of Philadelphia for £500 (English pounds). Three others bought 1,000 acres each! Some of these were Quakers, and some were Mennonites. They had about forty or fifty who sailed on the ship *Concord*, and about thirty-three of those adults were from Krefeld, Germany, near Holland. They each received a three-acre lot in Germantown, plus forty acres nearby. At that time, the main road in Germantown was an Indian trail. There were many linen weavers among them, and it is said they were already spinning flax within four months after their arrival. But there were other tradesmen too, such as tailors, shoemakers, locksmiths, carpenters, and tanners.

"Daniel Francis Pastorius, a pious Lutheran lawyer from Frankfurt, Germany, had arrived about six weeks earlier and he had already built a cave house by the time they came. He was hired as an agent, and helped to lay out the town. In 1691, he was chosen as mayor. When the school was built in 1701, he was the first teacher. He can speak at least five languages. As I said, there were some Mennonites with the first group, but they had no ministers and they soon worshiped with the Quakers. The only one who didn't was Jan Lensen, a linen weaver. But later in 1688, others arrived, including my father and his family. We soon were holding meetings together on Sunday and Dirck Keyser read a sermon from Jost Harmenson's book, and we would sing.

"But George Keith, the Scottish Quaker who was the leader in the Quaker schism, felt the Quakers were drifting too far from the Bible and New Testament. Many of the Friends were prominent men in the government and he felt they were not consistent enough against the use of force. Then there was also the issue of slavery. Keith thought no Quakers should ever own a slave. Already in 1688, a lengthy anti-slavery petition was written and signed here in Germantown among the Quakers, the first one in America stating in clear terms why slavery was wrong. It was sent to the monthly Dublin Meeting. The signers were Garret Hendricks and two brothers, Abraham and Dirk op den Graeff. These three were Quakers who had Mennonite backgrounds. Then there was Daniel Frances Pastorius, of whom I have already told you; he was the fourth signer. The monthly meeting turned it over to the quarterly meeting, they then turned it over to the yearly meeting, all in short words saying it was too touchy or too weighty a matter to make a decision. Abraham op den Graeff later joined the Mennonites again, and George Keith published an anti-slavery article in 1693, called *Slavery Opposed to the Golden Rule*. About ten years ago, William Penn asked the Philadelphia meeting to establish worship meetings for slaves."

Father cleared his throat, "Then this anti-slavery protest was the very first such protest here in America that you know of?"

"Well, no," said Claus, "not if you consider Cornelis Plockhoy and his colony. Most people consider Germantown as the first Mennonite settlement in America, but we have had some come here from

New York who had lived there for years, but they had no ministers and no church as such. But back nearly fifty years ago, about 1663 or so, a man from Holland by the name of Pieter Cornelis Plockhoy had lived for a time in a communal group in England. He wrote and circulated pamphlets citing the Hutterites, the Anabaptists of Moravia, and the communal way of life. He requested parliamentary support for such groups where poor people might settle, share goods, a special tax instead of military service, religious freedom, a democratic government, and no slavery or slave trade. In 1662, the Amsterdam City Council agreed to help twenty-five Mennonite families leave for Delaware. They settled at the mouth of the Horekill River on the Delaware Bay in a valley the Dutch had called Swan Valley. There had been a Swedish settlement there earlier, but the Susquehannock Indians had killed them. But they were caught in the vise between the Dutch and the British and their bloody battles for an empire. English troops captured all of Holland's North American settlements and lands, including New York. The commander of the English ship had been irritated by the resistance he'd met from the Dutch in recent weeks and he destroyed Plockhoy's settlement down to the last nail. We do not know what all Plockhoy might yet have accomplished had he not gone blind soon after. About thirty years later, he and his wife, both old and destitute, came here to Germantown. Father and another man, with the help of others, built them a small house to live in and helped them until Plockhoy died about five or six years ago. His had been a great dream and I've often wondered how it might have turned out if it hadn't been for the fighting that destroyed them. Most of them seem to have gone to other settlements, so they're all scattered now."

"Your father, William Rittenhouse, was he born in Holland?" asked Father.

"He was born in Mulheim on the Ruhr River in 1644. He was the only one of the family to become a Mennonite. His brother Heinrich was also a paper maker and his family worshipped with the Dutch Reformed Church. I believe they were apprenticed to the great paper maker Adolf Vorster, who took over the Mulheim paper mill in 1643. In 1679, he moved to Amsterdam; and then in 1688, he brought Mother and us three children over to New York, and then on to Germantown. It takes a lot of money to start up a paper mill. William Bradford, the King's printer, and two others put in shares, and then Father and I ran the mill. It's very hard work and Father was an old man long before his time. That same year we built Mother's small stone house. I remember what a time we had until we had that huge log was squared off and placed on top of the fireplace. I also helped to dig out the cellar."

"When was this house built?" asked Mother.

"Three years ago," answered Henry, the oldest of the boys, who had been quietly listening.

"Yes, and now I see that we should have built it bigger," chuckled Claus. "Wilhelmina keeps talking of adding another part, but I don't know when it will happen."

"You seem to be quite prosperous in your business by now," stated Christian.

"Yes, I must say we have been richly blessed, but for a time we didn't know what might happen. You see, this is our second paper mill. The first one was destroyed by a spring flood in 1700. If we hadn't been the only paper makers in the colony, we might have fared differently. William Penn was concerned and personally collected funds to help us rebuild. The new mill is larger, and we can make more paper than we could with the first one. We bought out the other partners as we could; it took us four years. When William Bradford fled to New York because he sided with George Keith in the Quaker Schism, we bought out his shares. But anyone who thinks paper making isn't hard work has never tried it. It's something you don't learn overnight either."

"I think I would like to go see the paper mill sometime," suggested Mother.

"I'll take you tomorrow," promised Wilhelmina.

"When was your father made a minister?" asked Father.

"At the same time Jan Neuss, who was a weaver, was chosen as a deacon, about 1698. It was at the home of Isaac van Bebber," explained Claus. "About four years later, Father wrote to Holland, asking for help in finding Bibles and hymnals. Also at that time we made arrangements for a burying ground. In 1702, Jacob Gottschalk and Hans Neuss were chosen as ministers as well."

"Oh, here comes Maria already!" exclaimed Wilhelmina. "It must be near suppertime."

As Maria walked toward the house, Mother asked Wilhelmina to tell her how Maria had come to live with them.

"She came across the ocean when she was eighteen," said Wilhelmina. "She had started seeing a young man and they felt they had no future in the Palatinate, so they both came over as indentured servants for five years. She has one more year to go, and we will help her start out by making a chest and filling it with linens and feather beds and such things, although many supply only clothes to wear. Her young man has been working in a brickyard in Philadelphia and his master will also give him a start. They plan to be married soon after their time is up."

"Do quite a lot of people come over that way?" wondered Mother.

"Yes, I think it was the year we came over that they said on one of the lists there were more than twice as many persons coming as indentured servants than free heads of households."

"It seemed Maria's greatest fear was that someone might buy one of them and take them so far from the other that they might never see each other for five years. They both attend the Lutheran church and after church, he walks out from Philadelphia. They spend some time together before he has to walk back. But Maria's a good, hardworking girl, and I think they'll do well here. A lot of those who were indentured only several years ago now own good property. Anyone with good health who is willing to work hard and be thrifty can better himself here in America."

The next morning they started out for the paper mill while Father went to see what was happening with the rest of the men. Wilhelmina showed them how worn rags were placed in the stream and fastened with rocks. "This washes the impurities from the linen and causes the fibers to break down. All buttons and hooks and eyes have to be cut off first. Then the rags are placed in vats of water to ferment and to disintegrate. We also get all the scraps from Germantown's linen industry, as well as from around Philadelphia. The rag men who collect rags in Philadelphia bring them out here. They sort them out and Claus pays for them. Then that water wheel turns the paddles inside. Come, I will show you."

Inside, Mother and Anna saw wooden paddles that rose and fell into large vats until the linen was a fine, white pulp. "Claus is doing the job of the 'vat man.' See how he takes what looks like a box with a sieve on the bottom and dips it into the pulp. He must fill it evenly with just the right amount of pulp, then he shakes it to get rid of the water. The next man is called a 'coucher.' His job is to drain more water from it, and then flip it on the piece of felt." They watched the "coucher" work, and Wilhelmina added, "It looks easy, but it isn't. If that isn't flipped over exactly right, it will fall apart."

The next worker took this and added another sheet of felt on top. "They do that until they have 144 sheets of paper on a stack. Once they have six stacks, they bring them over here to the screw press to press the water out." She showed them a great heavy-timbered wooden press with a massive wooden screw with two holes through it. "They put this pole through the hole." She pointed to a strong, round pole. "A man pushes on each side to press out the water. This puts great pressure on the paper. It takes strong men to push the pole to provide enough pressure. The felt is removed and the paper is pressed again. They then take it up to the loft where a worker called a 'lay man' hangs the sheets up to dry. That's a job that has to be done just right, too, or the paper will not dry right and won't lay flat. It needs to be turned when partly dry. Once it is dry, they size it to make it suitable for writing with ink." She showed them a finished sheet of paper. "Every paper maker puts in a 'watermark.'" She pointed to a finished paper that had the letters "CR" faintly outlined or pressed in.

"Does that stand for Claus Rittenhouse?" asked Anna.

"Yes, it does. If you will look, you will see that his molds have a wire with those letters in them. That makes the paper thinner there, and leaves a mark on the paper. When we return to the house, I will show you some of the other marks we used in the past."

Back at the house, Wilhelmina found a flat wooden box with several papers inside. The papers all contained Rittenhouse water-marks.

It was nearly evening when Father returned with quite a bit of news. The men had left in the morning to look for less expensive land farther west. They had taken with them Johann Rudolph Bondeli as an agent and guide. Seven years ago he had talked with Swiss agent Michel when he had visited the Conestoga Indians while hunting for "silver mines." Wendell Bauman went along as well as Hans Funk and Hans Groff. Hans Groff would have property to sell there if they liked what they saw.

The next day was cooler. The women helped Maria cut the squash from the vines and carry them to the house. The children carried them up to the loft where the visitors had their sleeping quarters. "We put them in here. Then when it gets cold, we pile them all around the fire-place chimney so they won't freeze. If we have more than we can store here, we bury them in hay in the cow barn."

"How do the Indians store them?" asked Father.

"They keep them as long as they can in the fall, but they also dry some. Sometimes the Indians cook corn and beans together. They call it succotash, and it's very good. I'll get Maria to make it one of these days. But the Indians also eat corn and beans and squash together. I don't care much for that, though I can eat it. They also have a way of making parched corn. Corn kernels are dropped into hot ashes. This sort of bakes the kernels. Then the ashes are sifted out with a basket. The corn is then ground into meal, which the Indians use when traveling. They mix it with water, or in the winter time, melted snow. To us it is not the best way to eat it, but the Indians will go on a long journey with only a small bag of this parched cornmeal."

"Do the people eat a lot of this Indian corn then?" asked Mother.

"A few do, but most regard it only to feed the animals. Once it is dry enough, I'll grind some for you. It tastes best when added to a bit of meat such as squirrel or rabbit."

Christian bent to pick up a stone in the squash patch and held it towards the sun. It glinted and sparkled in the sun.

"Does it look like gold?" Wilhelmina asked with a smile.

Christian grinned back at her. "It glistens a little like silver," he answered slowly.

"There are flecks like that in a lot of the rocks around here. Some people call it 'fool's gold.' It's really mica. I've heard that in some of the other colonies they filled several ships with the glittering earth such as you notice here on the path and shipped it back to Europe," smiled Wilhelmina.

CHAPTER SEVEN

Several days later, Hans and Christian showed up, brimming over with stories. They had apparently stopped first at the paper mill and talked with Claus.

"See what we've got here!" said Christian as he laid a leather bag on the flat stones in front of the house. He opened the bag and lifted a handful of rich, dark soil from the bag and let it sift through his fingers.

Father bent down and did the same. "Where did you find soil like this?"

"Oh, up towards the Susquehanna River near the Pequea Creek. Tomorrow we want to go back to Philadelphia to the office of the surveyor general and take out a warrant for 10,000 acres."

"Ten thousand acres!" Father and Mother gasped at once. "Whatever do you want with 10,000 acres?" asked Mother. "How do you expect to pay for it?"

Christian held up his hand for a moment. "As we journeyed together, we told the rest about the persecution of Benedict Brechbühl and the others from Bern. We came to the conclusion that we should take out a warrant for enough land so that others of our Brethren can settle around us. And we wanted to go far enough west from Philadelphia that such a large tract would be available. They told us William Penn will give us credit. We will be able to get it at a good price because no speculators will have bought up the surrounding land. They tell us that the speculators bought up the surrounding land around here and they would only sell one tract at a time. That way they could get a much higher price. Besides that, we want enough land for our children, too. And isn't this like the good, dark soil that Thomas Chalkley talked about? Oh sure, it will be hard work, and we know it will mean some hardships until we can build a mill nearby."

"What about the Indians?" asked Mother.

"We learned some things about them, too," replied Hans. "They had made a treaty with Penn in 1701, but there were problems since then. There is a village of Indians living near the Susquehanna River who are now called the Conestogas. Apparently, they were some of the remnants of the Susquehannock tribe who mixed with the Senecas. They had been conquered by the Five Nations of Iroquois to the north some years ago, and that is why Penn had been unable to make a complete treaty before 1701. He also was required to buy the land from the Iroquois of New York and asked the governor of New York to deal with the Indian leaders there."

"We also heard," added Christian, "that William Penn has 5,000 acres reserved for himself and his sons. It is located in the middle of Chester County, which reaches to the Susquehanna River. The nearest mill is about forty-five miles away at the Brandywine."

"Yes, and Hans Groff and Wendell Bauman went with us to look at the land. They liked it so well they are thinking of joining us," said Hans.

"Hans Groff said it's in our favor that James Logan, who is Penn's agent here, went to England just now. He's a very shrewd businessman. Now, we instead deal directly with the Quaker surveyor named Jacob Taylor. A young man from Germantown by the name of Bondeli, who traveled with us, will apply for the land."

Father nodded. "Very good, then. We'll purchase land for the persecuted Brethren if we can. May God provide."

Christian and Anna and Mother and Father talked again that evening. "Claus told me," said Father, "that we can dry all the apples we want. They are so plentiful that some are even fed to the cattle and pigs."

There was much to discuss when Claus came home from the paper mill. Father asked about the speculators.

Claus nodded, "Speculators . . . some want to get rich, others do us a favor. Wealthy people from England own most of the land around Philadelphia, some of whom are Quakers. William Penn only sells large acreages, so those who want only a few hundred acres buy from people who have the large tracts. Jacob Telner was Penn's agent to promote Quaker and Mennonite immigration. Penn wanted them as settlers. Telner and two others each bought 5,000 acres here around Germantown. Three Mennonites bought 1,000 acres each. Then others bought from them. In fact, some years ago, some Dutch Mennonites who had moved to New York but had no established church there came here to Germantown and bought small amounts of land.

"But to get back to the land . . . some of the land they had purchased was about twenty miles northwest of here. The van Bebbers bought some of that land as well as over 6,000 acres more from William Penn. Some called it Bebbers Township, but most call it Skippack. That's where the Mennonite Kolb brothers live. Their grandfather, Peter Schumacher, was one of the first ones to settle here in Germantown. He was an ex-Mennonite Quaker. In fact, there is a lot of mixing. My sister's husband, William Dewees, was of the Reformed Church. They live at Skippack. And Wilhelmina, my wife, was also of the Dutch Reformed Church in New York. We had been in New York first and I went back a year later, married, and then we moved here to live."

Father said, "I see. The way it looks, the Mennonites here at Germantown come from four separate places: Holland, Krefeld, Hamburg, and the Palatinate."

"That's right," Claus answered. "The Krefelders are primarily weavers. Most of the rest are tradesmen of some sort. A few are tanners. Quite a few of those who wanted to farm have moved to Skippack. The linen weavers, of course, grow flax. Here in Germantown, everyone was given a three-acre lot plus forty acres outside the village. But as you can see, both in Skippack and in the area outside of the village here, we have given up living together in a village, or *hof*. Each family builds a house and a barn which are not connected as they were usually done in Germany and Switzerland. And we don't have several families living together on one *hof* with the land elsewhere."

The next morning, Martin Kendig and Wendell Bauman stopped by. "We just got back from the Schuylkill," Martin said. "The Marcus Oberholtzers are staying there, you know, and are thinking of buying land there. We talked with others and they offered to help us clear land and build if our younger men all come up to help. They say if we have a late fall, we can do quite a bit this fall yet."

Both Christian and Hans nodded. "That sounds very good to me," said Christian. "I was itching to go up to the Pequea Creek area and just fell some trees, but knew we should wait until the land is surveyed. This will help us get some practice."

Martin added, "I've also received some news of the Palatines who sailed from London to New York last Christmas. Remember the Quaker who told us it was the wrong time of year for such a venture?"

Hans nodded, "I've often thought of them."

"Well, they didn't arrive until June 14 of this year." All of them gasped or stared in open-mouthed wonder.

There were several minutes of silence, then Hans said, "That's nearly six months. Their food couldn't have reached that long."

Martin sadly agreed, "I know. I learned that nearly half of them didn't make it." There were soft moans from some of the women, then Martin continued. "Well, not half, but 1,700 out of the 4,000 didn't make it. There were seventy orphans apprenticed to people from New York and New Jersey. At least they found a home and will learn a trade."

Again there was a stunned silence. Father took a deep breath. "I knew we were blessed more richly than we deserved, but now . . . now . . . once we know what life on a ship is like and to see others dying around you like that must have been very, very hard on the ones who did survive and they will never forget it as long as they live." He sadly shook his head.

After the two men left, everyone appeared stunned and sobered by the news that they had heard. Plans were made for Hans and Christian to leave for Skippack early the next morning. Wooden handles had already been made for their axes. Hans and Christian spent some time polishing their axe handles and Claus gave a jar of ointment to put on them. "It's beeswax mixed with turpentine," he said. "It helps preserve the wood and makes it easier on the hands—not so many blisters," he added.

On Saturday, two men appeared where Father was gathering walnuts. "We are Jacob Gottschalk and Hans Neuss," they said.

"Yes, I recognize you from the Sunday meeting," said Father, "but I don't believe I got to personally talk with you. Our sons said they did."

"We did not know there was a Mennonite minister among us, or we'd have asked you to speak. Would you be willing to take part at the next meeting?"

Father nodded. "Lord willing. It was so good to hear another sermon after so long. I needed that as much as anyone and was glad to listen. To gather together with others when we were homesick for the fellowship of our dear Brethren, to find new ones awaiting with open doors and giving, helping hands. To see the rich bounty here and apples more than we can eat. The sense of freedom one feels from others . . ." Father's voice broke as he wiped away a few tears.

Hans Neuss asked, "Is it true no one died on your ship coming over?"

When Father nodded, Hans said, "When I heard that, I wondered if it was true. That's why I asked you about it. Do you know I've heard that on the average, nearly one in five do not survive that trip."

Father agreed and related the story that Martin Kendig had told of the 4,000 who had sailed for New York and had taken nearly six months to get there.

They both shook their heads. Then Jacob added, "I've heard of things like that before, but usually it was just one ship, not four."

"Won't my German be hard to understand for those who are Dutch?" asked Father.

"I believe they can understand the German beter than your people can understand our Dutch. We have all been around German people much longer than you have been among the Dutch."

Father nodded. "We could communicate in Holland. It's not so different, but you Krefelders who come from the border between Holland and Germany are easier to understand than the ones at Rotterdam. And sometimes the sermons are easier to understand, the same faith expressed from the same Scriptures." There was a nodding of heads.

Father watched the men leave as he took the basket of nuts to the house. He saw two more men in the distance. Hans and Christian were coming! He opened the door of the little stone house. "Children, look who's coming." All day they had been asking, "Will Father come home for Sunday?" And Frances had had to say, "I don't know." Now little Hans and Fanny ran out to meet their father, shouting as they ran.

There was so much to say. Christian and Hans showed them the blisters on their hands that were already healing. Felling trees was hard work. The really large logs used for ship building were saved. They also had to dig out the stumps. It was more work but made better fields to produce better crops.

"One day it rained, so we helped flail wheat on the threshing floor," Hans told them. "I've been thinking of next spring. When I see all these new homesteads, I realize what all we don't have and what all we sold or gave away before we came. Martin Kendig said we should make a list of things we really need."

"Each family needs at least one bucket," said Mother, "maybe even more than one, and a few baskets of different sizes and a tub or two. And some wooden bowls, some rope, and we need to make handles for our shovels. Wooden rakes for hay, too," she added, then she chuckled. "Remember when the ships were being fixed and I told you about making hay on the mountains? I've remembered since then that I didn't tell you what it looked like when the men took the hay down the mountains. They had great big cloths like we use for tents and we'd pile the hay in them and then tie the corners together. It looked so funny. The hay piles were so big you couldn't see the men. It looked like those hay piles were slowly sliding down the mountains all by themselves."

There was a chuckle all around, then Anna asked, "Tents, don't we need tents for shelter until we can put up houses?"

The men all nodded, and Hans said, "Martin Kendig is asking about a dugout, like the first settlers made for winter. They told him they were too smoky. He asked if you couldn't add a chimney and they said one could be added, but it should be built into a south-facing bank."

"I was just wondering about that when you spoke of hay rakes. What are we going to feed hay to?" asked Frances.

"Somehow, we've got to get some cows. We'll have to have milk. And we'll need oxen too. If we can't get oxen, then a horse or two would come in handy. They're better for dragging logs; I saw that this week, but they do cost more," said Christian.

"Well," said Mother as she stirred the pot, "supper is ready. I cooked extra for tomorrow, so there is plenty. And we'll have all the apples we want. Come and see how many we've dried so far," she said as she showed them a linen sack. The men nodded in satisfaction and Father told of his visitors and what they had asked.

Christian and Hans both talked of the beautiful bright-colored trees that were everywhere and how the leaves were starting to fall. "Little Hans and Fanny were playing in the leaves all afternoon," said Frances. The rest nodded in agreement. Then they filled their bowls with a hearty soup that Mother had made from turnips, onions, beans, and parsley. There was only the soft glow and crackle from the big fireplace as dusk arrived. They could also hear the creek outside as the water tumbled over the rocks.

The little house seemed nearly full with six adults and three children in its one room. There were only two small benches. The men sat on the big chest and the children on a small one. There was a long silence as they rested tired aching muscles. After awhile Mother said, "There are no words to express the peace and thankfulness in our hearts. But, we do need to get the bed ticks out."

So the two young families climbed up the ladder and first handed down the bed tick for Father and Mother. Tomorrow was Sunday and Father wanted to get up as soon as there was enough light to read so he could read and study the Bible.

*   *   *

It was so pleasant walking together with Claus and Wilhelmina and their children to the meetinghouse in Germantown. The children joyously kicked the leaves and gathered a few brightly colored ones.

They were a bit early, so Claus and Wilhelmina used the time to introduce them to others. Christian swallowed as someone came and spoke his name, but Christian couldn't remember the man's name. "I . . . guess I must apologize . . . somehow I have no trouble remembering the name Kulp, but these Dutch names . . ." he shook his head.

The man smiled, "It's op den Graeff!"

Christian nodded in relief. "I'll remember the next time," he promised. They waited to go inside until a group from Skippack came. Most of them were on horseback.

Christian smiled a bit to himself when he noticed heads perk up when they saw Father sitting with the ministers. As they sang the first two songs, a few more came in whom he didn't recognize and he assumed they also came from Skippack.

Martin Kulp had the opening sermon. He touched on many points: our need of repentance when we sin the many blessings that come from God; and being thankful for the bountiful harvest. Then there was prayer. After the prayer, Deacon Jan Neuss read Matthew 5:1-25.

As Father rose to make his opening, he said, "Peace be unto you," and then waited as if weighing each word. "The peace of God and the love of our dear Lord and Saviour Jesus Christ who shed his blood for our sins be with you." As he quoted much from the New Testament and then went back to Old, he also told the story of the seven French warships; the great fear of many—who could be understood—even if one couldn't understand all the words that were being said. "Fear has a common language," he said softly. Samuel Guldin's bold words of faith from the Scriptures; The long, long night of prayers and yielding themselves into God's hands.

Father's voice grew softer as he slowly said, "The awe and the wonder of the next morning; the fog so thick they could hear people speak but they couldn't even see them; how they had to find their way about the ship very slowly so as not to get hurt."

Christian saw the hearers were spellbound and goose bumps were on his own arms as once again he himself remembered that brisk west wind coming up and yet the fog lasted for three more days; the French warships had disappeared; and the prayers of thanksgiving and praise to God that were raised as a result.

"I believe," said Father slowly, "that no one who has ever lived through something like that will **ever** forget it. How often, when our plans meet with another setback, do we become impatient? One such time happened for us on the ship. There was a bad storm, and for all of you who have been on a ship on the mighty ocean, I don't need to explain much about that." There were quite a few heads nodding in agreement.

"Well, there was such a storm," Father continued, "and several of the tall masts broke off, so you can have an idea of the severe storm that is was. We had to turn back when we were so eager to get here — back to an island where the damage could be fixed. Maybe we forgot to be thankful that we could still do that, that we were still at a place where we **could** turn back.

"While these repairs were being made, we gathered together at one end of the ship and talked . . . about Switzerland . . . about the martyrs and their faith and a lot about those who wrote most of our songs. Since then, different ones of the children who were among us have come and asked more questions about the things we discussed those three days we waited. Not only the children, but others also have spoken of those three days . . . of what it meant to hear these stories again . . . of suffering, hardships, and martyrs' deaths. How they were expelled with not more than the clothes on their backs. Even now there are those who are still in prison for their faith."

He went on to tell the story of Benedict Brechbühl and the rest of the Brethren who were shipped down the Rhine River in chains. He shared how they were delivered by the hand of God through the Dutch Mennonites.

"We need to tell these stories to our young men, women, and children...the stories of those who suffered and died for their faith.

Sometimes God sends trials as He did to those who were imprisoned in the dungeon of the castle of Passau so long ago. Who would have dreamed then that out of that damp, cold, dark cellar would come songs . . . fifty of them that we continue to sing today?

"Also," he went on, "perhaps those stories of faith, death, and suffering that we told while we waited for the ships to be repaired may have taken root in some young heart, that the cross of Christ may someday win us a crown. We are the spiritual descendants of those who suffered for Christ with their very lives. Was the ship's need for repair a delay . . . a turning back . . . or three days of idleness? Or was it God's way of showing us He still rules and can bring good out of calamity?"

Later, after a song had been sung, Christian listened to several different conversations.

"Yes, it was while William Penn was in prison that he did much of his writing. 'No Cross, No Crown' was written then."

"Yes, I was just a boy back in Krefeld when William Penn and George Fox, who was the founder of the Quakers, came on a preaching trip. Penn was a young man then."

"Yes, I've heard that George Fox was influenced by hearing a Mennonite preacher."

"Back in 1650 or so, because of persecution, Mennonite weavers went to Krefeld—an area with a little more tolerance. They soon had a thriving linen industry going there and through this the town prospered, much more than other towns around Krefeld. In fact, most of our weavers here in Germantown descend from those Mennonites. A Quaker missionary came through Krefeld and several Mennonite families joined him and started separate meetings. They no longer tipped their hats when greeted in the streets. Twice armed men expelled them. One was thrown in the street, kicked, and dragged by his hair until he was too injured to walk. Three years later, the Quakers had a chance to come here and they did."

"Yes, there were some Mennonites in Kriegsheim who also joined the Quakers. The Quakers opposed paying special taxes that the Mennonites had always been willing to pay. This caused the officials a lot of concern for these taxes paid their salaries. So seven of the Quaker men were jailed. This all happened in 1680. To pay the heavy taxes, the officials took eight cows. They took not only cows, but also sheep and pigs as well as cabbage and turnips."

"Even the turnips?"

"Yes. Besides that, the tax was higher than they had the means to pay."

"Yes, my grandfather talked about that a lot. This put the Elector on the spot. He needed those good farmers for the economic benefit. So in 1664 the Mennonites had to register or pay a very high fine. They were to be taxed six *guilders* a year as Mennonite Recognition Money. No more than twenty families were to meet for worship and no members of the official church were allowed to enter when they had meetings."

"But I still think that's why Grandfather Peter Shumacher left a year later and came to Germantown, even if Elector Prince Karl Ludwig had made some concessions. He knew they could be taken away again. It only took them two months to come over on the ship *Francis and Dorothy*."

Christian had to smile as he saw all the women from the ship in a close circle. After being together every day for so long, they really missed each other, Anna had told him. He saw his mother reach into her pocket and give Fanny and little Hans some dried apple *snitz*. They were hungry since it was well past dinner time.

Jan Lensen greeted Christian with the holy kiss. "Will you be heading back to Skippack tomorrow again?" he asked.

Christian nodded, "News must travel fast here."

Jan grinned and nodded, "Everyone is concerned, especially when you are new here. I'd invite you to our house for dinner, or would you rather wait till winter when it's too cold to be in Skippack?"

Christian sighed. "Yes . . . I . . . I think we'd like to spend the day with the family, if the invitation still stands for later?"

Jan nodded and Christian said, "They tell me you were the first Mennonite in Germantown in 1683."

Jan nodded slowly. "Yes, I . . . I could have done as many of the others did and join the Quakers, but I lived on in hope that more Mennonites would come and we could have our own meetings. It took so long, though—longer than I expected. But that's a long story; maybe it can wait for another time."

*   *   *

On Monday morning, by the light of the fire, the Herrs ate their breakfast of rye porridge and milk, along with apples, bread, and butter. Christian and Hans wanted to start the twenty-mile walk to Skippack as soon as it was light enough to see the path. Anna and Frances planned to walk with them for a mile or so.

"You know," said Hans, "I'm very glad we are returning to Skippack. We can learn so much from those new settlers that will be a help to us. Here in Germantown, people have built larger houses or stone houses and have things so much more like at home that it looks sort of overwhelming. Up at Skippack, most buildings and homesteads are only a few years old. It's simpler and we can learn lots of ideas about what we can do or what we'll have to do. I'm looking forward to these two weeks. Gerhart Clemens came over last year in the fall and the neighbors pitched in and helped him build a small house. Now he's about ready to erect a larger cabin beside it, with a bigger fireplace. They plan to work at it together this week."

"Yes, I'm looking forward to it, too," answered Christian. "We've helped build half-timbered houses at home, but here everyone builds log cabins because the wood is so plentiful and it's much quicker. We need to learn how to build them."

"Yes," said Father. "I've been watching carefully to see what I can learn, but it's much better to help build one and learn that way."

As Mother cut apple slices for the children, she asked, "But if Clemens wanted to put up a cabin, why did he wait until so late in the fall?"

"Because they were trying to clear as much land as they could to plant wheat. Once the wheat and rye is planted, were they able to take time to build the cabin. The other farmers had time to help too."

Father nodded. "The crops should come first, as long as they have a roof over their heads."

Hans opened the door. "I believe we can see well enough by now. Let's start."

The two couples crossed the Monoshone Creek on the footbridge and started on the trail together. The sack slung over Hans' shoulder contained their lunch: bread with apple butter, apples, and some of the walnuts Father had already dried and shelled.

The leaves swished under their feet as they walked. "Let's keep our eyes open for deer. They say dawn and dusk is the best time to see them," suggested Christian as a gray squirrel ran up the tree beside them.

"We'll have to learn to walk quietly like the Indians do," added Hans. "Martin Kolb says we'll need to purchase guns and learn how to shoot if we are moving into a new forest. He says wild game and fish, plus wild greens and berries are what we'll live on until we can raise a wheat crop, and that won't be until summer a year from now. He showed me the net or seine they use to catch fish. He also suggested that we purchase some traps to trap animals; not only for food, but their furs are a prime source of trade. At first I was disappointed we couldn't move up to the Pequea this fall already, but I can see now it will be very good for us all to learn more of the things we need to know to survive here. Martin said he'll try to teach me how to shoot this week."

Anna nodded. "Yes, I wish you could have found work in Germantown so you could be at home with us, but the skills we'll need to survive are worth a lot more than the money you could earn in Germantown."

After walking with their husbands for a while, Anna and Frances returned to the Rittenhouse homestead. They and Mother helped Wilhelmina and Maria gather the last of the fall crops, except for most of the root crops. Those would stay in the ground until the ground would freeze. Wilhelmina gave the women a basket of onions.

"We always plant lots of turnips," Wilhelmina told them, "and what we can't eat, the cattle get. We cut up the Indian squash for the cows, too, if there is more than we can eat. If the turnips are good enough for you, you are welcome to all you want. We had a good hay crop earlier this year so we don't need a lot of turnips for the cows."

"Turnips are what we lived on at home at times," said Mother, "that plus other crops such as parsnips, beets, cabbage, and sauerkraut."

"One of our neighbors has offered extras of those," said Wilhelmina.

It was with a deep sense of satisfaction that Anna and Frances worked to take onions up to the loft to store for the winter.

"Sometimes," said Frances, "when I think of all the things we need yet . . . it's hard not to worry. I've heard a bit of how hard it was for the first families here and that William Penn was generous enough to give them some food and supplies for the first winter. But no wonder they called it *ArmenStettle* (Poortown) if they had no one who helped them. The ones at Skippack said they've been given help from the older settlers here."

"I've been trying to think of a way to get a cow or heifer," said Anna. "What could we do?" As she pushed the basket of onions, one rolled off and stopped against the spinning wheel.

"The spinning wheel!" she exclaimed. "We've brought the main parts and only Mother's is ready to use now, but if we get Father to fix ours, we can spin for the weavers in Germantown. Let's ask him."

Father was out in the garden taking the ears of Indian corn off the stalks. The fodder was fed to the cows and some of the corn was fed to the pigs when it snowed too deep to find acorns in the woods. Claus had said they could grind some to eat, too. He told them the Indians lived on this meal most of the winter.

Anna shared her idea about the spinning wheels with Father.

"Yes, I've heard they have sent word that spinners were needed," Father said. "It shouldn't take long to get those wheels ready to go. I'll speak to Jan Lensen and see what he says."

CHAPTER EIGHT

Hans and Christian turned to wave to Anna and Frances before they disappeared into the woods, and then quickened their pace. The soil soon turned to a more red-brown color.. Soon they startled a flock of Indian hens. The next animal they saw was unfamiliar to the men. It was gray and had a smooth tail and a pointed head.

"See if we can describe it to Martin Kolb so he can tell us what it is."

"Keep your eyes open for a spring of water," said Hans after they had walked awhile longer. "We could soon use a drink and it will be quite a bit farther until we return to the Skippack Creek."

Christian nodded, "I'll watch on the left and you watch on the right side of the trail."

"Let's each eat one of the apples so my bag won't be so heavy," said Hans, as he got two apple s out of the bag and tossed one to Christian. Christian missed the apple, and a chipmunk scampered away in the leaves, dropping the hickory nut he'd been carrying. As Christian picked up the apple, he chuckled, "You may have the core of my apple once I'm done with it, little fellow."

They walked on in silence. Then Hans said, "Just look at that beautiful blue sky and white fluffy clouds. And see those hawks, how they soar!"

Christian squinted up at the sky. "There are six of them," he said. "They are so majestic and just seem to float in the air."

It was Hans who first spied the spring. As they stepped into the woods and cupped their hands to get a drink, Hans said, "Somehow I always have to think of Gideon and his brave three hundred when I drink like this."

"I guess we could lap it up like a dog if we had to," agreed Christian. "The sun is getting up there. Let me have another apple."

"It took us almost seven hours to walk home last Saturday. At that rate, it will be quite a bit after noon until we get there."

"Did you hear that Martin Mylin got work in a blacksmith shop and will start working today?" asked Christian.

"Is that right?"

"Yes, he's hoping he can earn enough to get tools and some iron to take along so he can make door hinges and nails and such things for the houses and also shoes for the oxen instead of buying them. We don't really have the money for that anyway. He'll have to make charcoal first, but of course there is plenty of wood available."

"Let's go up the big hill before we eat," suggested Hans.

"Have you noticed," asked Christian, "that there are really big trees in the Pequea area?"

"Yes, I noticed. Martin says the red soil here is good loam, but it has clay underneath and if it rains a lot in the spring, they can't plant oats early. Or gardens, either. It doesn't drain well."

Christian and Hans pushed up their breeches to cross the Skippack Creek. They were tired by the time they reached Martin Kolb's.

Martin's wife, Magdalena, served them some bread and cheese. "This fills us up well, Magdalena. Just what we needed," said Christian.

"Martin says you are to come over to Henry's. He just came last year and needs some more help. Do you think you can find it?" Magdalena asked.

"Last week Martin showed me the path you use and he said it is the next farm," said Hans. They got their axes and started out.

"Did you know," said Hans, "that Henry is the only one of the ministers who was ordained in the Palatinate?"

Martin saw them coming and greeted them.

"We'll work till dusk, then I'll head home. Henry's wife, Barbara, says she'll give you supper and you can sleep on the hay in the barn if that's good enough for you."

Both men nodded. Later, as they went inside for supper, Hans and Christian looked around the new cabin.

"How is it," wondered Hans, "that Gerhart Clemens got only a small house built last fall and you've got a nice-sized one?"

"Not everyone is blessed enough to have three brothers who prepared for your coming. They had the land picked out for me and cut quite a number of trees, plus they had gathered a lot of stones for the fireplace and cured mortar to use to set them up. We haven't gotten the floor to the loft in yet. I've split a bunch of boards, but Barbara wants them smoothed off a bit. So I'll be working with the drawing knife when the snow blows, if our plans hold. That's why you'll have to sleep in the hay," Henry explained. "Tomorrow is the cabin raising at Gerhart Clemens," he added.

"We're really looking forward to it," Hans said.

"You can expect the whole neighborhood to be there. It's been a real nice warm fall so far. His wife was getting a bit worried that we might not get the cabin built before it turned cold, but we've had only a few cold snaps so far."

"Does everyone have a dirt floor?" Christian wondered. "I noticed that he Rittenhouses have brick floors."

"Most of the farms start out with a dirt floor with a hole dug in a corner and covered with boards as a cellar for food storage," Henry explained.

"What about the windows? Are they very high priced? Anna was wondering about that," Christian added.

Henry sighed. "Yes, my brothers helped me buy these or we'd have had to wait. We paid them for them with the furs we trapped last winter."

He went on to talk about his crops. "I've got three acres of wheat and rye planted that are growing nice. We put in a little rye last fall. That can be planted later than wheat. I'm hoping it will keep us in rye bread for the winter. The straw was used to thatch the barn roof."

"You spoke of trapping," Hans said. "We—we seem to need so many things and don't have the money to buy them."

Henry got up from the bench and stretched. "Someone can take you to the store in Philadelphia where Brother Jacob got mine. He gave me the traps; then I used the furs I got to pay for them later. Between the windows and the traps, there was very little left over. But we always hope for next year, to have more left over."

"Oh, by the way," said Christian. "We saw a gray animal with a smooth tail and a pointed nose on our walk here this morning and we didn't know what it was."

Henry chuckled heartily. "That must have been an opossum. They have a little pocket in front to carry their babies and they can play dead and then disappear later. You can eat it. With animals like opossums and raccoons that have a musk gland under the front legs, you must remove it if you want to eat them. My wife adds some garlic or else onions when she makes them."

"Yes," said Barbara, "that's one thing I've learned over here is that we use a lot more onions and garlic when cooking wild animals or roasting them in the oven. It improves the taste a lot. I also use dried parsley, and if I'm short on salt, I use herbs such as sage and thyme, along with the onions and garlic."

As Hans yawned, Henry said "I'll show you where the hay is stored. I'm sure you're tired after your long day."

Christian left his arms hang loose. "Yes-s, we are. But we also feel so thankful and blessed in many ways. I . . . we . . . we sort of feel like little boys again . . . who have so much to learn."

Henry cleared his throat and nodded. "I believe I've learned more in the last year or so than in the five years before that. And I still have a lot to learn."

The next morning they tried to get an early start, but even so there were several men there ahead of them. A middle-aged man, who Henry said was Lenard Henricks, seemed to be going ahead. He was using a colored twine to snap lines on the logs. After each snap, he'd put the twine back in a little box and shake it.

"What's in the box?" asked Hans.

"Lime mixed with pokeberry juice. That's what makes it a purplish color. Now we'll take the broad axes and square off the one side to make the inside wall," Henry told him.

As they worked side by side, Henry informed Hans who each man was. Today it was not only Mennonites who helped. There were English and Scotch Irish and Germans, who were Lutheran and Dutch Reformed.

"There comes William Dewees, the brother-in-law of Claus Rittenhouse. And I'm sure you know Marcus Oberholtzer and George Miller," Henry chuckled.

Hans wondered, "What kinds of logs do you use?"

"Any kind. We use hard woods for the lower logs, such as walnut, hickory, oak, or even maple. For the upper logs, it's not as important. The hard woods are heavier to lift up. Oh, and poplar is plentiful too. We use that mostly for the upper logs."

"I see Gerhart has his chimney up already. It is big and looks good."

"Yes, you can also put up the chimney later if you wish, especially if you build as the English or the Scotch Irish do. Around here they say you can spot a German home from a distance because the fireplace is in the middle of the house. Most non-Germans put them at the end of the house."

Hans said, "But if you put them in the middle, it warms up the whole house much better." Henry nodded in agreement.

Lenard Henricks gave him some advice about building his chimney right. "Many a settler didn't know enough and found they had a chimney that wouldn't draw and the house filled with smoke."

"Mmm . . . I've heard Father talk about that. A chimney won't draw if it isn't built right, but I'm not smart enough to know the difference," Hans replied.

"Once it's dinnertime, I'll take you in and show you what I mean. Others who knew how to do it helped me, or ours probably would have smoked too," Henry said.

"I see he has a small stone foundation set up about a foot or so and the small house behind it looks like the logs are down on the ground. Why is that?" Hans wondered.

"The little house is just resting on some stones dug in every so often. It was the quickest way to do it. But the ones at Germantown that were built like that have mostly been replaced or repaired, because when the stones settle, the logs start rotting much quicker or the termites make more trouble too. You also asked about a dirt floor. The women are planning to someday dig out a cellar inside the house and set up a stone wall. Then you can put floor joists on the stone wall, and a floor on top of that.

"There's one house here in the settlement where they did that and now all the women decided it would be a good idea. More than one family has begun collecting stones or cutting logs to split boards. At least they can dream about it. We actually plan to close the loft off, and work on the ceiling. We wrap boards with straw dipped in mud and cow dung and plaster over that so it's easier to keep warm. At times we were pretty cold last winter," Henry told him.

Christian could soon see that there were others there who'd had more experience using a broadaxe than he'd had. Lenard Henricks was now marking the places for the notches on the logs. Christian watched a bit, and then said, "I've noticed that some of the houses in Germantown have squared-off logs and dove-tailed edges."

Henry nodded. "Yes, someone said there are as many ways to build a log cabin as there are people who build them. The squared-off logs take a lot longer to do and it is not easy to get those dove-tailed correctly. Maybe you noticed that there are also some houses in Germantown that have board siding. Most of those have logs underneath that were dove-tailed when they were put up, not with the ends sticking out like we poor farmers do."

Christian agreed. "Yes, I'm not saying I don't like the ones in Germantown, but somehow these seem to fit into the woods better. They look so cozy and homey to me."

"I like the way you said that, cozy and homey, as if they were a part of the forest," Henry said. "Our German villages were very nice, too, but with the land and fields scattered . . . I like it much better this way, with each person's land all together and close to the barn. Over there, we spent so much time getting to the fields and a lot of time getting the crops home."

Soon the men were ready to start setting up the logs. Henry and Christian each took one end and Martin Kolb and William Dewees the other end. It fit right in. Lenard Henricks had done his measuring well.

"I see your wife is here now, too," said Christian to Henry as he saw several women around a large kettle over a fire.

"Yes, she had soaked some beans to put in the pot today. We usually don't eat till the loft joists are on, and sometimes if all goes well, we get the side loft logs on and then prepare for the roof after we eat. Each woman usually brings her plates and spoons so there's enough to go around. Here, with it being all new homesteads, we don't have lots of apples like they do at Germantown. In the fall when we farmers take wheat to market, we usually fill up a few of our wheat bags with apples from a relative in Germantown. I doubt that's something you can do up your way. You'll have to eat lots of apples this fall and winter because it will be several years before you can grow your own."

"I hadn't thought of that, but the women are drying a lot. I believe I've eaten as many apples in the few weeks we've been here as I did in several years at home. For one thing, we were so tired of ship's fare that we were extra hungry for them. To me, I think that picture will always stay in my mind of our welcome to America. We were so-o-o hungry for fresh things; it was like outstretched arms of welcome to be given those apples and peaches on the Delaware River, and from complete strangers at that."

"Someone **remembered** what ship travel and ship fare was like anyway," agreed Henry.

Soon they needed the help of all the men to add the floor joists.

"Why are they leaving such a wide space between the one and not the rest?" asked Hans.

"That's for the ladder to go up to the loft, or as wide as that is, it's big enough for stairs, if they ever want to add them. They've had time to check out all the cabins in the settlement and decide what they want."

Once the floor joists were on, Christian saw Lenard Henricks look at the sun. "Let's try to get the loft logs all on until noon if we can."

No one had noticed that one of the boys was using a small ax on a short log that he was trying to notch, and soon a cry was heard from one of the other boys. Blood was running from a wound in his thigh. The boy was Richard, the seven-year-old son of an Englishman.

"Do you have some yarrow?" the boy's father asked Gerhart Clemens.

"Yes, I think my wife has some dried yarrow."

"Don't bother hunting it; I've got some along," said Lenard Henricks, as he went to his tool bag and got out a leather bag. "I always take some to a raising in case someone cuts himself."

As the boy's wound was exposed, he let his father pack the wound with the yarrow to stop the blood flow. "An old Roman soldiers' remedy," said the father, as it stopped the bleeding and he wrapped his handkerchief around it.

The father said, "I've heard it's been said that it was used in the crusades and that the Romans always carried it to the battlefield with them. They learned it from the Greeks. It prevented many a soldier from bleeding to death and italso seemed to help the wounds heal better," said the boy's father. "Some people call it 'wound wort.'"

The men were soon back at work again. Christian noticed that the logs above the loft floor were smaller and seemed to be poplar logs.

According to the sun, it was a bit past noon when the men went for dinner.

"Let's pray," said Henry Kolb, as the men took off their hats and caps and bowed their heads for a few moments of silence.

Christian took a spoonful of the soup the women were dishing out. He didn't know what kind of meat was in the soup, but he guessed it to be either wild goose or duck by its appearance. Turnips, onions, peas, beans, and parsley had been thickened with a bit of flour. Mmm—it was good. There was also fresh bread with apple butter and a wooden platter of cold, sliced, cured ham, along with apple dumplings and pies made from the Indian squash like the Rittenhouses had made.

Hans remarked, "This ham here, it tastes a bit different and is very red."

Jacob Kolb chuckled, "You've just had your first taste of bear ham. I got a small bear about six weeks ago and salted and smoked all the hams. We poor farmers don't have much luck with porkers, as the bears like them too well. So we make ham out of bear, or you can also cure the deer legs, too, just as you would pork."

"I haven't noticed many sheep yet, either," said Hans.

"That's the wolves' favorite, just like pork is for the bear. In fact, I've heard that one sign there is a bear about is nervous hogs. But it's getting better. Around Germantown, they can have sheep and pigs now, and there are fewer wolves and bear around here than there were when the first settlers came."

Hans sighed. "That means we'll have to give up our dreams of having our own hams and bacon and wool for spinning for a while."

The men nodded. "But you can dream about it, just like the women dream about wooden floors and big cellars like they had in Germany or Switzerland."

"Well, at least here you don't have to worry over how . . . just how . . . you are going to pay the taxes," someone said.

There was a gentle murmur of agreement and Christian added under his breath, "Or that the magistrate or the constable is coming to fine you or put you into prison." Again, there was a murmur of agreement.

Lenard Henricks looked at the sun and got up from the log he'd been sitting on. The rest of the men took the signal and rose too.

"Let's get this roof on."

"Gerhart, are you sure you counted your rafters right?" one of the men called out.

Gerhart pretended not to hear, and Jacob told Christian, "When we put up the barn, Gerhart was short a few rafters and we had to go chop a few saplings down so we could finish the job."

Christian watched as the squared-off plate was put on top of the logs, which had holes drilled into them with hand augers, and pegs were pounded in and then sawed off. The rafters had been squared off and were mortised at the ends, with holes drilled and ready to be pegged. They had been notched to fit over the plate. Once a few rafters were up, a board was tacked on with nails to steady them until the lathing was put on.

"Let's clean up a bit here," said Jacob as they started to clear the center of the house of wood and pieces, "so if someone drops a nail, we can easily find it."

Christian sighed. "You know, Jacob," he said, "I can already see that there is a lot more work to building a cabin than I'd thought. I'd heard talk of putting up a cabin in a day and, yes, it looks like that can happen, but just being here and . . . well . . . seeing all the work that was done ahead of the building, like the rafters and the plates . . . and the debarking. Why do they do that anyway?"

"So you don't have trouble with the bugs. Bugs get in under the bark, and not only that, when it rains, the bare logs dry off better. Sometimes they even do the work with the broadaxes ahead of time like we did today.

"Yes, you can build a rough cabin in a day or a week, if you don't care how long it lasts. I've seen such rough ones and the logs settled down or one twisted or what we call rolled or turned. Soon the roof starts to sag somewhere and after awhile it leaks or is hard to keep warm because the logs won't stay in place and the chinking won't stay tight.

"There is no reason a well-built log cabin can't serve for your children and maybe even your grandchildren too. That's a choice you need to make. Do you build a good one and make improvements on it as you go along, or do you build one for a few years and then build a better house later?" Jacob explained.

"And the cost! I can see already we'll have to do without windows, not the nails for the lathes and the shingles. It'd take time to make nails and we won't have rye straw to make a thatch roof either," Christian said.

"One way I've heard of putting on shingles is to put a longer sapling on each layer and tie a weight on each end of the sapling to keep it in place."

Hans nodded, "That way you could use the shingles again later somewhere else. I'm thinking of a shed or lean-to, for temporary shelter," he added.

"Good idea," agreed Jacob Kolb.

The women had cleared away the dishes and now came with baskets. They gathered up the larger chips and the small pieces of wood and put them in the baskets.

Some of the men were mixing up the chinking. As they put some between the logs, the smaller pieces of wood were placed in the wall with the chinking.

"Why the pieces of wood?" asked Hans.

"It makes it stay in place better and of course, takes less chinking that way. See here, you can help, just so the wood pieces don't show. Always be sure the chinking doesn't come out as far as the logs, especially at the top or the rain will come in."

Hans nodded, "Today I'm beginning to sound like my own little boy . . . Why . . . Why . . . Why?"

Meanwhile up on the roof, the lower line of shingles were being put into place. The children were instructed to be ready in case a nail fell down.

"Why did they extend the plates so far?" Christian wondered.

"To give the roof more overhang at the ends and sides. It protects the logs more from the rain. Not every cabin is built that way like the little one in the back there."

"Yes, I see," nodded Christian. Suddenly he thought of the fireplace. "Your brother promised at dinnertime to show me how you have to build a fireplace so it won't smoke."

"Well, you can see it here if you get inside and look up."

"See here," pointed out Jacob, "this smaller part a little above the mantle level is called the throat of the chimney, or some may call it a baffle. You need to be sure the opening at the top is not smaller than this opening at the throat, or your chimney will smoke. There was a fellow not too far from our place who had to tear the top part off and rebuild it to make it larger. Then it worked fine."

Christian took a deep breath. "I see, it's very simple if you follow that rule."

"Yes, that's it . . . no cheating."

He watched the rows of shingles being nailed. They were handed up one by one by the boys for the first row until enough were laid. After the first row was laid, they could use a rope to pull up packets of shingles and lay them on the new roof.

A while later, as the men prepared to go home, they looked at the day's work and nodded their heads in satisfaction. Christian cleared his throat.

"I . . . I have a question for you. You all know by now that we will be going back into the woods forty-five miles from the nearest mill. Do you have any advice for us?"

There was a strange silence. As Christian waited, he felt his knees become a bit shaky.

"We heard a lot of good advice last Sunday at the meeting," one ventured at last. "We're poor ones to give advice when we need some so badly ourselves."

Christian wanted to say a lot of things but felt too stunned and tongue-tied to say anything.

"Well, pray for us then," added Hans weakly. There was a nodding of heads as the men gathered their tools to head for home.

"Gerhart!" called Martin Kolb. "A few of the men and most of the women haven't heard the stories old Hans Herr told at meeting on Sunday. How about gathering here after an early dinner and let Christian and Hans tell us the stories he told us about their trip over and the Brethren who are persecuted in Bern."

"Agreed!" said Gerhart after he'd looked at his wife and she'd nodded her head.

After they had started for home Christian and Hans both looked back at the cabin for several minutes.

"Look! He's started a fire in the fireplace!" exclaimed Hans. As they watched the smoke rise up into the sky, it made a beautiful picture in the setting sun.

"Snug and cozy-looking," said Christian wistfully.

"I wouldn't have built it there," said Hans.

"Why not?" asked Henry Kolb.

"I'd have built it up near the Pequea if I'd been building it," he said with a smile.

Henry laughed and they started for home at a brisk walk. "I believe Barbara's supper will be ready when we get home," he said.

CHAPTER NINE

Back at the Rittenhouse homestead, Wilhelmina was feeding the geese some Indian corn. She explained to Anna and Frances, "We've found that if we feed them corn in the fall before we butcher them, it fattens them. And goose fat is good for baking as well as many other things."

Anna told her of their plans to ask Jan Lensen for spinning. She nodded. "There's a flax break out in the barn, but we don't use it any-more. I just get my linen from the weavers in Germantown. If you ask around, sometimes there's someone who has extra flax stalks that they don't have broken or heckled yet, and they'd probably let you have them. The weavers always like to have extra on hand."

"You mean Father could break it for us and heckle it too, then we could spin it?"

Wilhelmina nodded. "Most of the parts of my mother's old loom are in the attic too, if someone also wants to do weaving."

Anna's eyes gleamed. Father had a small loom, but Christian and Hans had never learned how. Eagerly they went back to tell their father-in-law the news. He said, "I was just ready to go see Jan Lensen. Let me get my heavy coat out of the chest. It's a little colder this morning."

It was nearly dinnertime when Father came back carrying bundles of flax over each shoulder. His coat was hanging open because the day had gotten warmer.

"I've got good news for you. Jan says the weavers can always use extra spinners. He's also got a heifer that should freshen in 'hay month' (July). He'll take his wagon and see what he can collect for us. That way we can be paid directly for every bobbin you do." He took a bunch of bobbin sticks out of his pockets.

"*Gott sei dank!*" (Thanks to God), said Mother.

It was late afternoon when Jan Lensen came with a wagon piled high with flax stalks. "Most people I asked for gave several shocks, so here's a lot of work for you. Now if you want to earn a little extra, and someone has the time to collect walnut shells and dye it, so much the better. I'm also quite sure with this late fall we're having you can still gather pokeberries that will give you a dark red or purplish color, depending on how much you use them. I can always get indigo down at Philadelphia for you to make the blue. I do mostly blue and plain linen together for tablecloths; also dark red and plain; and then some plain brown, as well as brown and plain. For bed covers, it's mostly blue and plain. It's up to you if you want to dye your own or not. This house has a larger fireplace than most, so you can dye over winter if you've got a large pot. But if you'd rather just do the spinning, I can take it to the dyers in Germantown."

They discussed all that Jan had told them. Then Father said, "Why don't I take little Hans and Fanny and we'll go see how many poke-berries we can gather. I did save the walnut shells that I've already picked up. But we could use more hickory nuts and walnuts too. Why don't we collect some while the flax is laid out on the grass to get brittle enough to break. That shoulf take about two weeks. Jan brought us three bundles that are ready now to put through the breaker. Since the weather is still nice, we can collect more nuts and berries until the rest is ready to break."

The next day as the hickory nuts were placed in front of the fire-place to dry, little Anna took some of the nuts and placed them in a row, put a stick between them, and then started another row. "These are my 'briths,'" she said. "I'm making a 'brith' floor."

The women smiled and Frances said, "Yes, Anna, you may make a brick floor."

On Thursday evening, Anna was listening to the flop-flop-flop of the flax break outside as all three spinning wheels hummed. The Rittenhouse children were outside, watching and asking questions.

"Doddy Herr," asked Henry, "why did you lay all the flax on the grass?"

Father explained, "You see what falls on the stones here?" He picked up the short stems lying on the stones. "That is the inside of the flax plant. These fibers that almost look like long hair are the outside of the plant. Because the stems got brittle from a lot of soaking or being wet, they break when I put them through this flax break. Here, take a few stalks and see if you can do it too."

Henry tried a few and smiled as the stems fell on the pile. Father grinned back at him. "I suppose a little boy who already knows as much about paper making as you do can be forgiven if he doesn't know much about flax."

"I've seen them heckle it though," added Henry. "Can I try that too?"

"Get the heckle," Father told him.

Henry came with a piece of wood about three inches wide and about six inches long, filled with spikes about four inches long.

"You've got the wrong one, Henry. That is the fine-toothed heckle. First we put it through this big-toothed heckle. See what comes out?" He showed Henry what was caught in the heckle. "This we call the tow. It's what we use to make the bags to put the wheat in and also for tents or if you need to cover things on the wagon."

"My father has one like that. Look, here comes a wagon. It's Uncle William's horses, black and brown!" he shouted with glee and ran off to meet the wagon.

Several minutes after the horses were in the barn, the excited children came leading the man who'd come on the wagon.

"I'm William Dewees," he said. "I took a load of wheat to Philadelphia and my wife Elizabeth thought it would be nice if I brought the women along back to Skippack with me."

Frances' mouth fell open and Anna took a quick deep breath. Before anyone could answer, little Hans and Fanny chimed, "I want to go too. May I go too?" As they danced up and down, Father answered, "Thanks for the offer. We'll talk it over, then let you know how many want to go along."

William nodded, "I'll have to warn you though, some of you may have to walk up the hill." There was a nodding of heads and bright smiles and William chuckled at their eagerness. "You can see whose hearts are at Skippack just now."

William went on to say, "There's another farmer at Skippack who wants to bring a load of wheat in on Monday morning. He'll bring you back, but you may have to walk part of the way."

Later Father said, "Mother and I talked it over, and while we'd like to visit the Skippack sometime, all of us would be too many to come back with a load of wheat. Mother and I might try our hand at dyeing what you've spun this Saturday while the house is empty. In fact, if it's warm enough, we'll do it outside. We can use vinegar as a mordant to set the dye if we don't have enough salt."

It was barely daylight when they started off, with the women and children crossing the Monoshone on the footbridge while William went down to the ford and crossed there. He soon caught up with them as the horses were fresh and seemed to know they were going home. A few bags had been filled with apples and the rest of the bags had been folded up to make nice cushions for them to sit on.

The leaves had mostly fallen by now and the group could see far into the woods. "Are you dressed warmly enough?" asked William as he noticed that Anna and Frances each had a child wrapped in their cloaks. They both nodded and William said, "It will soon warm up when the sun gets higher in the sky. I expect to be home before dinnertime. The men are at Henry Kolb's this week instead of Martin's, so I'll take you there. He lives on the farm next to Gerhart Clemens, where we put up the cabin this week and where we'll get together again on Sunday."

"You mean you'll have meeting there?" asked Frances.

"Not really. Every four weeks we have meeting at Skippack, and then in between we go to Germantown; those who can go, that is. Sometimes the women take turns keeping the children or they take the wagon and go on Saturday already, and a neighbor will milk their cow for them. But when we gather on the in-between Sundays, we always sing for some time. Like on Sunday, Henry announced we'd gather at Gerhart Clemens' new cabin. You can probably expect to meet the whole community there. Most times it's just a few families here and a few there. Because Martin asked your husbands to tell the stories of your trip over and of the persecutions of the Swiss Brethren . . . well, I expect some of the Reformed and Lutheran neighbors will also be there. Sometimes a few even attend when we have meeting, as most times they only have visiting ministers, or else have to go to Germantown for their church services. Oh! Look ahead there—"

There on the trail stood two doe and a bigger buck with a large rack. They looked at the horses for a second then bounded off into the forest.

"They're beautiful!" exclaimed Anna.

"Yes," agreed William. "I believe everyone would agree with you. They're so graceful when you see them bounding away. They seem to sort of sail over every obstacle. But deer were the primary source of food for the Indians, they say. I've heard the Indians were very angry when white people first came and shot deer just for the hides and left the meat to rot. To the Indians, that wasn't right and showed them that the white man had no sense."

"That wasn't right," agreed Frances and Anna.

Once the horses slowed down, Frances said, "Anna and I will take turns walking now if you'll stop to let us off."

"Just up ahead here is a spring where we let the horses drink. I'll walk awhile myself to stretch my legs," William told them.

"Can I drive the horses?" asked little Hans.

William nodded, "I'll walk alongside and you may drive."

As they walked up the trail after their stop at the spring, Anna looked at the picture it made: William walking beside his horses and little Hans holding the lines, with Frances and Fanny walking behind. *Maybe someday . . . that man would be Christian with our own wagon,* Anna thought.

When they came to the hill, everyone walked except the two children as William led the horses. They each ate an apple and William said, "When we cross the Skippack, we'll soon be home."

*   *   *

For quite some time, Hans had been chopping at a large oak tree. The three men were working some distance apart, so if one felled a tree, the others were not in danger. He looked at the sun once more.

His stomach was telling him it was dinnertime. Hopefully he could fell this tree yet before Barbara blew the Alp horn calling them for lunch. The oak was almost ready to fall. He made a few more strokes and looked up at the top to see if it was swaying . . . no . . . not yet. Then he looked back to where Henry was chopping . . . and caught his breath. There came Barbara . . . and a woman and three children and they waved at him!

Suddenly Hans felt like leaping like a deer as he bounded over to meet them. The children came running to meet him and flew into his arms. *"Dat!" "Dat!" "Dat!"* (Father), as Frances and Hans exchanged happy smiles over their heads.

"We surprised you!" cheered little Hans.

"You sure did!" his father agreed.

"I told them not to come over, as I saw your tree was close to crashing and it could be dangerous," said Frances, "but they were too excited."

Hans nodded as he saw Christian and Anna come walking together. Christian was all smiles. "Looks like our planned horseback ride for next Saturday won't materialize," he grinned.

"Yes, we'd each planned on riding home on borrowed horses next weekend, but this is so much better," agreed Hans.

"That means you can help one more day here," said Henry.

Just then a little breeze came up and Henry told the children, "Watch that tree . . . see it swaying. . . ." and suddenly with a mighty crash, the tree came thundering down, shaking the ground where they were.

"That is one lesson all pioneers must learn," he said. "Beware of falling trees! They could be mighty dangerous!"

Together the group walked back to the cabin. "We saw three deer," said Fanny importantly. "They can jump fast."

The wives told of William's offer and how they'd enjoyed the ride. They also told them of the flax they were spinning, while Henry told them of the planned meeting for Sunday.

"It's good I just baked bread this morning," said Barbara.

After dinner, Henry and Barbara spoke quietly together and then Henry left.

"You go out and visit awhile. I'll do the dishes," Barbara told them. They protested weakly, but Barbara shooed them out the door.

After a while Henry came back. "I've been over to Gerhart Clemens," he said, "and we did some planning. We've been working your men so hard their pants are wearing out." Both women nodded and he continued, "For work like this, you really need leather breeches. I've only got one deerskin on hand, and a few other smaller ones. But Gerhart says they've got most of one left. So if you are willing, Christian and Anna can go over there for the night and hopefully you can get a pair of buckskin breeches made to take the place of the ones he wore out helping us here."

"But maybe if it turns cold soon we can't help much longer," protested Hans.

"Oh, we've already planned some more on that," smiled Henry. "If you can get someone to make a good buckskin coat and line it with smaller animal furs, and make a good pair of mittens, you can work in all but the coldest weather. Here, I'll show you what Barbara made for me last winter." He went to the bedroom and they heard him opening the chest.

He came out with a fur-lined buckskin coat. The mittens were longer and fur-lined too. He showed them how the mittens fitted back over the coat sleeves. "This you'll need to go hunting in cold weather," he said as he showed them a fur cap to match. "I also have fur leggings for when it snows. Out in the barn, I've started a pair of snow shoes of sorts—I hope to make better ones." When he saw their blank stares, Henry said, "It's something the Indians made to walk on top of the snow."

Barbara said, "We'll cut Hans' breeches this afternoon, then you can take what's left of the deerskin along over to Ann Clemens." She explained that Ann was a Reiff, whose people had lived at the Ibershiemerhof, and before that, they had come from Zurich. "She'll be so happy to meet someone from the Palatinate. Henry told her that Christian and Anna will be over for supper and the night. Then maybe he can help at the cabin yet or whereever he's needed tomorrow."

*   *   *

Ann Clemens gave Anna a kiss of welcome and shook her hand heartily. She was eager to meet someone who had come from the same general area she had lived. While they had never met personally, they knew quite a few of the same people.

Ann showed Anna the new cabin and the youngest of the three boys who was taking a nap. "This is our son Abraham," she said. "As soon as I found out on Tuesday that the meeting will be here on Sunday, I told Gerhart we'd have to get it cleaned out and the floor evened up a bit better. We had to put some water on the floor, so it will settle the dust and have time to dry out before Sunday. We won't move in before Sunday, but you and Christian can sleep here in the bedroom. Gerhart was pleased to have Christian come to help. Then they can finish the chinking in the upstairs. He has to use the ladder on the upstairs and it saves him so many steps if he has someone to lift the heavy buckets of chinking to him. Then maybe I can help you with breeches."

On Sunday, as the families were finishing up their meal, the first wagon drove in.

"Take the benches over," said Ann crisply, "and if more people come than there is room on the boards and benches you've made and the logs you've carried in, then we will use big fireplace logs yet. You can carry them in if we need them. Just so everyone has a place to sit. I put the bedtick in the corner for the babies to sleep on. Maybe I should get an extra pail of water from the spring for drinking."

"I can do that," offered Anna.

"Jacob can do that," she replied. "Here," she told her eight-year-old son, "if you boys go outside to play, be sure to keep an eye on John and Abraham."

By the time they had the dishes done, there were people coming from every direction, some on horseback, some in wagons, and many walking.

"Show me who Elizabeth Dewees is," said Anna. Ann pointed her out and she and Anna went to greet her.

"Are you Anna or Frances?" asked Elizabeth.

"I'm Anna, and I want to thank you for arranging this."

"The men planned last Sunday to loan horses to your husbands so it wouldn't take so long to get to Germantown, but we women wanted to meet you too. Unless we go with the wagon and stay overnight, the women don't get to 'meeting' in Germantown unless you've got a horse to ride."

Soon they were inside singing. How it warmed Christian's heart, as the beloved songs of the cross, the blood of Christ, forgiveness, suffering and trials, and heaven, and God's love over all rose in the new cabin so many had helped to build. It seemed so fitting . . . sort of a consecration of the new home.

Then, before he realized it, or was ready for it, he and Hans were asked by Henry Kolb to tell the story of the persecuted Swiss Brethren and the trip over. "One of you can tell the story of the Swiss and the other the trip," said Henry.

"I'll take the Swiss," said Hans.

"Stand up, so we can all hear," said someone from the back of the room.

Hans rubbed his hands a bit nervously and said out loud, "Where shall I begin . . . I . . . I . . ." His voice trailed off.

"How about with Benedict Brechbühl's visit," suggested Christian.

"About ten years ago or so," Hans began as the murmuring in the room grew quiet, "we were blessed to receive a visit from a gifted and zealous minister from Bern, Switzerland, by the name of Benedict Brechbühl."

Hans, sometimes haltingly but with lots of emotion told the story of this minister's persecution, the arrests, the prison, his property being seized to pay the fines, being expelled, in hiding, yet never wavering in his calling of preaching the gospel of Christ and ever concerned over his *folkli* (flock).

"The sentence of being expelled to Carolina without his family . . . the journey down the Rhine River in chains . . . the deliverance by the hand of God through the Dutch Mennonites . . . starting fast for home and being sent back to Amsterdam . . . and being forced to promise not return to Switzerland."

Christian noticed how everyone in the room was focused on what Hans was saying, even the boys were listening, some standing just outside the door.

"We have also received word since, through new arrivals, that Benedict was since ordained to be a full elder or bishop at Mannheim this summer. His flock plan to go to the Palatinate area of Germany somewhere, the way it sounds," Hans said.

Suddenly Hans sat down and somehow Christian's legs seemed extra heavy as he tried to get up. He took a deep breath. "I . . . I hardly know where to start either. Was it the high taxes and the special taxes because we were Mennonites, the French troops coming to destroy and pillage, the fact that the local people wanted our farms and were therefore somewhat jealous of us, feeling that we were Swissers and they felt we didn't really belong there. Was it the fact that we had to gather in only small groups? Or the chance for a land of plenty and freedom to worship, but all together, as all the rest of you here did too, we pulled up our very roots and made the decision to cross the vast and dangerous ocean. There's a feeling that I believe all of you understand, that of leaving loved ones behind. We left an older brother and two younger ones there. It wasn't easy!"

There was a nodding of heads; a few of the women wiped away tears and blew their noses.

"And yet, I've found a brotherhood here . . ." and a nodding of heads followed as he cleared his throat again, "a brotherhood of the same faith of caring, sharing, people — with open hands and hearts. As I think of what all we would have missed here, if my plans had worked out. For you see, in my dreams, I had plans of living in our own cabin now already. I had visions of shooting a deer whenever I needed one. But God saw we had need of learning many things. You see, I had chance to shoot a deer this week . . . and I missed it!"

There was an instant murmur among the men. "It was certainly good that wasn't my only source of food, for I'd have gone hungry!"

He went on, "We made our plans to leave early in the spring. All of you, too, probably met some delay along the way. . . ."

"We were becalmed for ten days," said one.

Christian nodded, "So you can understand when at first it was four weeks at London, then soon it was six weeks, and it was good we didn't know ahead of time it would be **ten weeks**.

"When we were finally aboard the ship, in the first hour, we hit a small boat . . . a boy drowned . . . then crashed into another ship . . . lost our captain because of the crash . . . storms so bad the masts broke off. . . ." Again some nodded.

"We had to turn back . . . that seemed so very hard in my mind . . . all the delay and then to turn back once more. . . ." He shook his head and many of the group seemed to understand. "But during those three days of quiet . . . at least no flapping sails, no creaking ship, we asked the older people about our homeland. They all told us stories of Switzerland. Stories of persecution and prison, of unwavering faith, even unto death. The songs we sang today took me back . . . back to those days of when and how these songs were written. Looking back now . . . those three days of calm were precious days," and he told them more about that time and the dungeon at Passau and the martyrs.

Then he told of the fear from the warships. "I once heard a saying, 'It was so thick you could have cut it with a knife.' I'd always dismissed such a saying as an unworthy exaggeration, but for many . . . yes, their fear made me think of such a saying."

It was so quiet as he softly started to tell what happened and his voice broke and he wiped away a few tears. . . . "The fog was so thick. . . . God had answered their prayers. It was so humbling, and yet so great and glorious too, something we will always remember as long as we live."

"Being becalmed brought fresh fish. The whales . . . is there anyone here who did not marvel and could hardly comprehend the vastness of the ocean or how big the whales were?" Again there went a murmur through the crowd.

"Then after arriving offshore on the Delaware . . . and the apples and peaches seemingly like welcoming open arms. And now, I'll have to confess, the other day when we had the cabin raising, I asked for advice and was very disappointed I didn't get any. I told my wife about it this morning, and she said maybe you didn't understand what it was I wanted and needed. She said she'd overheard Father and Mother talk about our brother Abraham, who didn't come along because they had several small children. Father said if we advise them to come and things don't work out, then they'd feel guilty about it. I suppose that's why you didn't have any for us. Anna said I should have asked about mistakes you made . . ." Christian was interrupted by many chuckles ". . . or lessons you learned." There was a vigorous nodding of heads.

Someone in the back quipped, "How late do you want to stay?"

Martin Kolb spoke up, "I learned to always take a rawhide rope along to drag a deer home and another to tie half the deer up in a tree in case it's too big or too far to drag the whole thing home. That way it won't be eaten by the next morning."

"The first summer my neighbor saw all our Indian corn and asked, 'Surely you don't have a squaw living in that cabin?' Well, we got quite a bit of snow, too deep to hunt much and he came to see if we had food. He was mighty glad for that 'squaw corn.' So the first year at least, plant enough corn to last all winter, until you've got a wheat crop. You can grind the corn yourself if needed."

"I learned to always keep salted smoked meat on hand. Even if it's only a 'coon or a 'possum in case it snows or rains too much to hunt."

"I learned to **never, never** get between a mother bear and her cubs, especially if you are armed with only an ax!" There were more chuckles.

"I learned, and the hard way at that," one said forcefully, "never to throw a stone at a skunk." A wave of laughter followed. Hans and Christian looked puzzled at the laughter.

"You need another introduction to a new animal besides the opossum," said Martin Kolb. "A skunk is a black animal that resembles a cat, but has short legs and a wide white stripe, often on its head and on the back. It's got an unusual defense. It sprays at anything that it fears may harm it. It's . . . well . . . I'm not sure how to describe the smell. It's very strong; very, very strong!"

"If one gets you, your wife will smell you before she sees you!"

"Yes, and you can sleep in the barn a few nights."

"You'll know it once you smell it."

"But skunks are excellent mousers. If left alone, they seldom make trouble. They won't attack; just keep a safe distance and let them alone."

There was silence for a few minutes, then someone said, "We learned the hard way that it's better to spend half a day putting up a fence for a toddler than to spend half a day hunting one." Again there was a murmur of agreement.

"Plant apple trees as soon as you can."

"Teach your children how to find their way home and to keep to the trails when they are not in their own woods that they know well."

"We marked some trees with whitewash. The children must stay within the tree line that has the whitewash marks."

"Learn the animal tracks and signs and how to stay upwind of a deer."

"Shoot the bucks first, doe only when no bucks are around."

"You can smoke and dry fish like the Indians do."

"Yes, that was something I wanted to ask about. What can we expect from the Indians? How should we treat them? What shouldn't we do?" asked Hans.

Someone replied, "The golden rule."

"An Indian may walk in quietly before you are even aware he is around."

"They like bread, especially warm out of the oven. And they'll trade. One took two loaves of bread and several days later came back with a pair of moccasins for my wife. She wears moccasins ever since."

"The Indians have no sense of ownership as we know it. Food belongs to everyone. The land belongs to all the Indians. Don't try to lock your door on them."

"Learn a bit of their sign language from someone who knows it."

"They like buttermilk, and sour milk too. And they know a lot of medicine using plants and roots. Our child was sick and an Indian came with roots and plants to make a tea. Our child soon got better."

"Someone has seen them gather mullein and the roots of a purple daisy-like plant and they also use the bark of some trees."

"Always keep some yarrow on hand in case of wounds."

"What about wolves?" asked Hans.

"Never leave a calf outside overnight. A wolf or a mountain lion may get a calf."

"Since you'll be forty-five miles from the nearest mill, get at least one horse to go to the mill. And get at least one bull."

"If you make your homestead near a spring, you won't have the extra work of digging a well."

"Be sure you know where you put your tools. We once spent half a day looking for my ax."

Christian and Hans thanked them for all the help they'd given them. Christian cleared his throat. "At the cabin raising, none of you wanted to bear the responsibility of telling us what to do, because you did not want to feel responsible if things didn't work out for us. We asked then for your prayers and you agreed. I think . . . I believe . . . what we should have said that time was 'Yes, we want your prayers. We surely need them. But this is one of those times when we need MORE THAN PRAYERS and we thank you for giving it"

There was a general nodding of heads as many rose to leave for home. Conversations started everywhere as people slowly drifted outside, visiting as they went.

That evening after they had all left, Anna said, "I had felt sort of guilty to take two days off from our spinning to come here. Now you're

getting a new pair of leather breeches and we've learned so much that
. . . well . . ."

"It's priceless!" Christian finished for her.

Anna nodded. "I like this new cabin. One of the women gave me
an old basket full of onion sets for us to plant next spring. It makes me
eager to plant. She said she plants extra seed and gives the onion sets
to new settlers. This should be enough for all of us," she said as she
lifted the basket.

"I've been thinking," said Christian. "It's so humbling to need
so much help and yet maybe it's also a lesson for us. The ones here say
the people from Germantown helped them, now both are helping us.
We can't do much in return. But we live in hope of having the persecuted Swiss and others settle among us. This shows us what we'll need
to do for someone else in the future, Lord willing."

Anna nodded.

Christian asked, "Did I tell you we are to work for Andrew
Schrager next week? He came over on the same ship as Henry Kolb
and Gerhart Clemens. He's in his fifties and has two single daughters."

Anna yawned and Christian laughed. "You're right! It's time to
turn in. We've had a full, but very good day."

CHAPTER TEN

It was six weeks later that all the Herrs walked to Germantown on a Sunday morning during a light snow. Everything looked so crisp and clean and beautiful.

"You know," said Christian, "I'm really looking forward to today. Jan Lensen is the only Mennonite who was there when Germantown was started. We've come to know him quite well through the spinning, and I've got a lot of questions again that I want to ask him."

Father chuckled. "So do I. I believe he realizes it or he wouldn't have invited us to come this morning."

"That's so we have time to sing and to talk, too," suggested Mother.

When the family entered the house, they marveled at the fat goose roasting on a spit in the fireplace. Jan saw everyone looking at the goose and smiled. "Yes, we killed the fatted goose if not the fatted calf."

"We've been looking forward to this for awhile," said his wife.

"Yes," nodded Hans, "we too, but now we've gathered so many more questions."

Jan chuckled. "Then maybe we'd better get started with our singing so we have time for all the questions because I've got a few of my own. Doddy Hans, we'll let you pick the first song."

After a number of songs had been sung, Father asked, "Just how long were you over here until you had meetings. How long until you had ministers?"

"Well, you see, there were only Quaker meetings here and at times I would go there, but never joined. Most of those Quakers were from Krefeld and were ex-Mennonites so we had the same background. In 1687, some of the van Bebbers came over, followed by two businessmen from Amsterdam. One, of course, was papermaker William Rittenhouse, who built the house you are living in. The other was a Mennonite silk merchant, Dirck Keyser, who sold Amsterdam-dyed silk. By the way, Keyser's grandfather was one of the signers of the Dordrecht Confession of Faith in 1632."

"Oh, he was?"

"Yes. In Germantown we met together in the van Bebber house and endeavored to instruct one another. Sometimes Dirck Keyser would read a sermon from a book by Jost Harmonsen. Of course, we would sing, too. Dirck had lost two wives and a daughter named Johanna passed away while they were coming here from New York. She was buried on the way. He did bring two sons with him. More Mennonites kept coming and because we had no bishop, we did the next best thing. We chose two by election: William Rittenhouse as minister and Jan Neuss, who was a weaver, as deacon. But we did not want to lose the church authority we had had. Since we had no bishop, we could not have baptisms or communion.

"In 1700, more families came from Hamburg, possibly about thirty people. This gave us a link to Hamburg and there was correspondence between the Germantown-Hamburg and Amsterdam congregations. The families from Hamburg were not satisfied with what they found, and wrote about their concerns relating to ordinations, baptisms, and communion. Could a bishop come from Hamburg and ordain a bishop at Germantown? Would that be possible?

"In the meantime, William Rittenhouse was trying to get the eighteen Articles of Faith in the Dordrecht Confession translated into English and printed by the church at Amsterdam. But nothing happened and no one here had the money to pay for it.

"About March 1702, the church at Hamburg wrote back and said, 'It is too far and too difficult to send a bishop. Pray earnestly for a season that the Lord would look graciously on the preachers there and overlook the weaknesses in them to enable one of them to take up the bishops' role.' They told of how Philip had baptized the Ethiopian, even though he was not a bishop. They sent a copy to the Mennonite leaders at Amsterdam, who kept it.

"With that go-ahead, two additional ministers were elected in October of that year: Jacob Gottschalk, who had come over just that year, and Hans Neuss, a brother to Jan Neuss, the deacon.

"The Rittenhouse paper mill had washed away and the owner was rebuilding, but he sold property to Deacon Jan Neuss in hopes of building a meetinghouse. However, neither of the two new ministers had the gift of public speaking and usually just read at meetings.

"There was also the matter of four different backgrounds and home congregations. It was new, uncharted ground and there were disagreements, just as William Penn's government affairs had a lot of difficulties the first years. Somehow, Hans Neuss, the new minister from lower Rhineland and Arnold van Fossen from Hamburg couldn't agree on certain matters, and Hans decided to leave. He left not only the ministry, but the congregation as well.

"That was hard on everyone," Jan sighed sadly. "Matters rested there for another five years.

"Meanwhile, people were moving to Skippack, Pennsylvania. This was another problem for Mennonites. William Penn had given the Germans at Germantown a charter granting the right to be self-governing and make their own laws. At first I felt it was a good idea but soon changed my mind. Pastorius was our mayor and was a gifted man who spoke five languages and was our first teacher.

"We Mennonites were willing to serve as fence inspectors but refused to serve as constables. I had even kept an inn for a time, but then was asked to serve as a committeeman in the town government.

I did not feel right about accepting such a position. Jacob Gottschalk also asked to be excused from jury duty. Claus Jensen and Hendrick Sellen, both Mennonites, had the thankless task of collecting a special tax to build a better jail. Abraham op den Graeff, who had signed an anti-slavery petition, was often involved in disagreements and once sued a neighbor. As you can see, we had troubles just as Penn did, except ours were much smaller.

"Because so many were buying land, sometimes two people claimed the same land. Some Lutherans sued each other over who owned Manatany (Pottstown). I had some differences with Jan Strepers, a large landholder,; but we chose to let others make the final decision about the land.

"William Penn's agent and overseer, altered the account books to show that Penn owed the agent a large sum of money. He had learned that Penn signed papers without inspecting them. When the agent died, his widow sued William Penn, who was put in debtor's prison for months until Penn finally managed to get a mortgage from a number of wealthy Quakers. Imagine, owning hundreds of thousands of acres of land and being in debtor's prison!

"In the meantime, the crown cancelled the William Penn charter for Germantown and the dream of German self-government disappeared in smoke.

"But three Kolb brothers wanted to come to America. Their older brother, Peter, was a bishop. Martin, Johannes, and Jacob, who was still single, immigrated here.

"Again there were questions directed to the Hamburg congregation regarding what to do about the lack of a bishop. The ministers at Hamburg wrote about the counsel they had given five years earlier and asked that the letter be signed by the Hamburg and Amsterdam congregations, because they had hesitated to accept our counsel. They wrote the letter on April 16 and signed it.

"Then Palatines immigrated here: the Kolbs, Wyands, and Bowmans, who were more conservative. None of them would have dreamed of wearing a blue silk coat as our silk merchant did, even if they had the money to buy one. This group worshipped by themselves for a year.

"Martin Kolb's first wife had died, and before too long he married Magdelena van Sintern. Martin's brother Jacob married Magdelena's sister Sarah and they began to worship with our congregation.

"William Rittenhouse felt great joy when he received the letter from Holland. However, a little more than six weeks later both he and his wife were struck by a fatal illness and died soon after. Therefore, it fell upon Jacob Gottschalk to act. There were several ordinations and three were ordained deacons: Isaac van Sintern, Hendrick Kassel, and Conrad Jansen. A month later, on March 22, 1708, two were made ministers: Herman Karsdorp, age fifty, and Martin Kolb, age twenty-nine. Now there were church leaders from all four places of origin.

"A log meetinghouse was built. On May 9, 1708, eleven persons were baptized and two weeks later we had our first Lord's Supper together as we heard about the suffering and death of Christ. That was last year, twenty-five years later for us as you probably know. Another Kolb brother, Henry, was ordained in the Palatinate before he immigrated to America with about seventy others. Many of those chose to homestead in the Skippack area and elsewhere."

"I see," said Father. "You followed a rather rocky path lacking leadership—like sailing on uncharted waters."

"Yes," agreed Jan, "but we feel our prayers have been answered; it just took a lot longer than we had first thought."

He sighed. "For awhile, one had to wonder if it would be the same here as it was in New York. The Dutch Mennonites there either moved to Pennsylvania or were absorbed into other congregations in time."

Jan rose. "I see that my wife is putting that goose on a platter. I believe she was preparing some special things for you all week."

As they were eating goose along with bread, butter, and apple butter, Father said, "I . . . I can better see now why you struggled. . . . We felt we were too old to start over in a new land, but we couldn't see our children coming over here without any ministry. We hoped someone younger might be willing, but God was gracious. The storms weren't easy for anyone to go through while we were on the ship, but we felt so blessed that we all survived. But now . . . to get started here. . . ." he took a deep breath and sighed.

"Yes! Yes, I sure know the feeling. We worked hard, and four months after we arrived we were already weaving."

Christian cleared his throat. "We've heard you and different ones say that you were so poor that people called it the town *ArmenSthettle*, the Village of the Poor. But why," he asked, "were you so poor if you were weaving so soon?"

"Ahem. . . ," nodded Jan. "The answer to that riddle is other people were poor, too. That was a lesson we had to learn—the hard way. No matter how good a product is, if people have no money to buy, or you can't get it to market, well, you're stuck. Of course, we could sell it if we made the price low enough. That kept us poor for awhile and we didn't know if it would get better. But once Philadelphia grew and merchants arrived who had money or things to trade, we soon did much better," he explained.

"In other words, what you are saying is that if we go to the Pequea Creek or Conestoga Creek area and raise good wheat, unless we have a way to get it to market we'll be in the same boat you were."

"That's right! You won't survive long either by trying to bring your wheat in on horseback. You'll need wagons, a road that wagons can travel on, and horses to pull those wagons."

"That means we'll have to turn at least forty-five miles of packhorse trails into roads," said Hans as he took a deep breath.

Everyone nodded their heads as the idea of clearing forty-five miles for a road sank in. Several of them sighed, then fell silent.

They ate mashed turnips and dried beans with the roast goose, along with pickled red beets. For dessert there were apple dumplings made with molasses and spices.

Jan's wife said, "Sugar here is too expensive. When the time comes that you can begin trading wheat, you can get small barrels of molasses from the West Indies. Philadelphia does a lot of trading with the West Indies which is said to be just off our southern coast. Since sugar is so highly priced, molasses is more affordable."

Christian cleared his throat. "While we were at Skippack, we asked all the new settlers to tell us lessons they had learned or mistakes they had made."

Together, he and Hans went down the list of suggestions, then asked, "Do you have anymore to add?"

"I do!" said Jan's wife. "Let one of your group train with someone who makes pottery. Crocks and other crockery are what you will need in order to store food, such as milk."

"Or sauerkraut!"

"Yes. I suppose you could store sauerkraut in barrels, but crocks are not practical to take on horseback or carry." There was a nodding of heads all around the table.

"Here we could trade linen for crocks and other items from Philadelphia. Where you are going you cannot do that."

Again there was a nodding of heads and silence for a bit as each thought about the information they had been given.

"I would also suggest some training with a wheelwright so you can later make wagons and carts."

Then Father asked, "You spoke of all the troubles that William Penn had. We were wondering about that."

"Which do you want to hear about?" quipped Jan. "The troubles in this country or the ones back in England?"

"Well, both I suppose or aren't they related?"

"Yes, I believe most of them are. In fact, the problems in England helped make the problems here, and Penn should have been both places to straighten them out. The ones here were exaggerated and used by those in England to undermine Penn. As you probably know, the King of England owed Penn's father a great sum of money, which the King didn't have to pay back, so he gave him a vast grant of land instead. Because Penn had become a Quaker he dreamed of a place where Indians and Whites would treat each other as brothers. Penn wanted to have a place where the poor and the persecuted could find a land of peace and prosperity. I do feel there's no better place to live than here, even though we struggled at first and some were homesick for a time. But about some of the problems here, I believe if Penn had stayed in America most of the problems could easily have been solved by Penn himself. He was wise, fair, and respected. In the first ten years here, there were six times of change in administration or form of government. Under such conditions, things didn't run smoothly. No one knew who was in charge of what. This caused more problems and dissatisfaction multiplied.

"Thomas Lloyd, a Welsh Quaker, was the strongest force, whether in active government or behind the scenes. He was educated at Oxford, had a lot of ability, and was of a strong character. Had he not declined the office, Lloyd might have become governor in 1688. Lloyd's services to the colony were great and important. Penn depended on him and trusted him as a great friend.

"There were two main governing bodies to make the laws, the council and the assembly. Each tried to have the most say in matters and felt they were the most important and should have the most power. For awhile it was like two roosters trying to rule the barnyard. This ill-feeling continued for several years and hurt Penn in England, because his enemies magnified the stories.

"King James, II, who was Penn's good friend, was expelled from the throne by the Revolution of 1688 and William of Orange landed in England.

"When Lloyd declined the governorship, Penn gave the office to a soldier, Captain John Blackwell, whom Penn hoped would restore harmony.

"People here did not understand Penn's problems at home and resented an officer ruling over them. The Quaker governing class were displeased with Blackwell, and possibly Blackwell resented this. He felt he had the upper hand and could impose his will on the people.

"Blackwell soon got into disputes with the assembly and other leading men including Thomas Lloyd. David Lloyd who was clerk of the Supreme Court at the time, was imprisoned on a charge of neglecting to deliver records to Blackwell. There were other problems and Blackwell became so disliked that the people demanded his recall. Reluctantly, Penn agreed and power was returned once again to the council with Thomas Lloyd as president.

"Then the lower counties became dissatisfied. They felt they did not get their fair share of appointments, but the root of the problem seemed to be the faster growth of the Pennsylvania counties and they feared being overshadowed by them. They had been here first.

"Reluctantly, Penn agreed and appointed Thomas Lloyd deputy governor of Pennsylvania, and William Markham, deputy governor of the lower counties. This lasted until 1693 when Penn lost the governmental powers of his colony.

"It didn't help that at this time the Quakers had a bitter split, called the Keithian Schism. George Keith, for a time the headmaster of the William Penn Charter School in Philadelphia, questioned areas of Quaker law enforcement, such as sheriff. He raised questions of conscience, not only for Quakers but for Mennonites as well. Many Mennonites were in sympathy with Keith.

"Here in Germantown there were some brothers on either side of the split. Keith printed a strongly-worded pamphlet and he and his printer got into trouble for it. The printer was even arrested. Keith had quite a following at one time, most of whom eventually were permanently lost to the Quakers.

"Keith soon left for England and was ordained there as an Anglican missionary, which of course, was the Church of England. To the Quakers this was too much. When Keith returned to America and tried to preach at their yearly meeting, the Quakers put him out on the street.

"In England, this whole matter added fuel to the fire of those who wished to take away Penn's governmental powers. In 1688, William and Mary came to the throne of England. Penn's close relations with former King James, II, was the cause of Penn being accused of being part of a plot to restore James, II, to the throne. When no evidence could be found to prove it, the charge was dropped, but Penn was still under suspicion. The charge that his administration was a failure was used to take away his power to govern. Later it was felt that Penn should return to help run things here. Unfortunately, Penn did not have the money to return to America and William Markham was again appointed.

"When William Markham tried to put into effect Penn's promise of more defense, the Assembly insisted on first having a new Constitution giving them greater privileges and power. The Assembly finally won some important issues. To be more responsive to the public will, it was known as 'Markham's Frame,' and limited the power of the governor without the consent of council."

"In other words," said Christian, "no governor could make laws on a whim that were against most of the people's wishes, and no one could do something such as Blackwell had done by imprisoning someone he disliked or disagreed with."

Jan nodded. "It was, of course, adopted with the understanding that Penn could overrule it. But once Penn returned in December 1699, he eventually approved it.

"After some debate and clashing of interests, a new constitution was adopted in October 1702. It was known as the 'Charter of Privileges' and reflected more of the will and freedoms of the people. These freedoms and privileges seem to have made the government much more stable and the people better satisfied.

"Other issues arose that caused trouble for Penn. Lord Baltimore of Maryland claimed some of the lower counties of Pennsylvania and Connecticutt claimed some of the upper counties. Then some businessmen decided to purchase 30,000 acres in western Pennsylvania around Lake Erie so they could capture the Indian fur trade from Canada and the west, and bring it down the Susquehanna River.

"The governor of New York informed the crown about this matter. New York was getting this fur trade and to the crown this was an important source of income. They couldn't let Penn sell the land and take away their income. Once again, Penn had difficulties and the venture had to be dropped."

Father cleared his throat. "This Keith split among the Quakers seems to have raised some good points that were not in line with either Mennonite or Quaker non-resistance."

Jan nodded slowly. "I've often wondered if the outcome might have been different if it had been approached in a different way," he said sadly. "Keith was so forceful in his speaking and writing that perhaps he showed the wrong attitude. Whatever it was, if he himself had remained true to all the Quaker teachings later . . . I don't know . . . but it sure caused a lot of ill feelings. I guess that's Satan's work.

"That brings me to questions I wanted to ask you. The Jacob Ammann split somehow—well, suppose you tell me what you know and heard. By the time the stories arrived here, it was hard to be sure. About all I've heard was that there seemed to be failings on both sides."

Everyone nodded to that, and Father said sadly, "Yes, I believe we can all agree to that."

After rubbing his hands slowly together for awhile, Father began. "Jacob was the son of Michael Ammann and was born and christened in the Reformed Church of Erlenbach in the Simmental Valley south of Thun. Both he and his father were tailors. When he was converted to the Anabaptists in his mid-thirties, it brought the threat of a flogging by local authorities. They later called him a 'roving arch-Anabaptist!' He could barely write and signed only his initials. His brother Ulrich did write quite a bit. I've heard he was also a very gifted speaker.

"In the ten years or so after he joined the Anabaptists, Jacob was ordained first as a minister and then as an elder or bishop by Hans Reist of the Emmental. He moved north and included the larger Alsatian community north and south of Thun in his circle of visitation and preaching. Ammann had a strong personality and great zeal, but he seems to have also been impulsive.

"In some of the older Swiss congregations especially in some of the issues of the Dordrecht Confession of Faith, such as shunning and foot washing, the issues were treated with caution because they had earlier caused conflict among the Holland congregations erupting into several splits.

"Hans Reist called Ammann a young man when, in fact, he was almost fifty. I believe because Reist had ordained Ammann, he saw himself not as an equal of Jacob Ammann even though both were bishops. Reist seems to have felt that the son should accept the advice of the father and obey him. I wonder if Ammann sensed this and was resentful. Perhaps Reist really meant he wasn't a bishop for a long time. We don't know for sure. But there was a lack of respect shown for Ammann's concerns, or so we felt.

"That may have helped Ammann to react as he did. One of the Palatine ministers remarked that the Dordrecht Confession was not on the same level as the New Testament. Ammann also was concerned about the question of dress.

"Ammann had started holding communion twice a year. He was sincerely concerned that the church was becoming too lax in Christian ordinances. He seems to have mistakenly believed that the Swiss Brethren had once kept the avoidance of ex-members the same as the Dutch Mennonites did because they had signed the Dordrecht Confession of Faith in 1660. He felt they had dropped it, but I could find no history to support this.

"The Swiss had never practiced this the same way as many of the Dutch did, perhaps partly because this had caused many divisions in Holland. The Brethren in Switzerland and Germany had been taught to use temperance and lowliness when practicing avoidance. Jacob Ammann and his followers wanted this practice kept more strict as outlined in the Dordrecht Confession."

"Wasn't there also a question of the truehearted people," asked Jan, "or the half-Baptists?"

"Yes. Those who risked prison, fines, and beatings for sheltering or hiding the Anabaptists, yet were not members; in fact, many owed their freedom to them."

Father sighed. "I can only say that God will be the judge. He sees the thoughts and intentions of the heart."

"Were there people in your area involved in the split?" asked Jan.

"Some of our ministers went to the Conference and pleaded with Ammann to let each follow his own convictions. We had sympathizers on each side." He shook his head. "So we heard both sides. The congregations involved were mostly centered around Alsace and Bern, Switzerland. You must realize that these people had all been hardened by years of persecution, and to have someone oppose them was nothing new, only this time it came from within and brought a lot of heartaches with it.

Father nodded. "As I said before, Reist did not seem to consider Ammann's concerns in the light he should have. Ammann visited all the ministers in Switzerland and called a meeting, but Hans Reist did not come, saying he was too busy with the harvest. Later Ammann again invited Reist to a meeting, but again he did not come. I wonder if Ammann would have reacted as harshly as he did had Hans Reist not treated him the way he did and warned the other ministers not to take this younger man and his ideas too seriously.

"In Reist's congregation, there was also a woman who admitted she had lied. Ammann felt that Reist treated this matter too lightly when Reist didn't come to the second meeting that Ammann had called.

"Ammann reacted rashly to this by excommunicating those who did not agree with him, including Reist. When the other ministers pleaded with Ammann to 'call a council' of more leaders from a wider area so that there would be no division, the response was that they too would be expelled if they did not agree with his proceedings. He then left without the customary shaking of hands.

Later there was another meeting in March 1693 with seven ministers from the Kraichgau including leaders such as Jacob Guth, Hans Rudi Nägeli, and about twelve leaders from Bern. Ammann explained his points, and it almost felt as though our ministers would have been willing to yield to Ammann; but those from Bern did not agree.

Jacob Guth proposed that Ammann and his followers could follow their convictions as long as they did not impose on others who felt differently. If that was possible, Guth said that they could accept them as brethren, and pointed out Scriptures to back this.

But the next day, Ammann and his followers did not come to the meeting and about sixteen ministers signed a paper placing Ammann in the ban. This meant that each side had expelled the other side.

"Reist seemed to have resented the manner in which the issue was handled, so much so that about five years later when the Amish realized that they had made mistakes too and hoped to unite once again, Reist did not respond. They even went so far as to put themselves in the ban for their rashness, which they now recognized. Ammann and his people offered to keep the principles as they understood them, and others could be exempt. Ammann was now willing to do what our ministers had asked five years earlier. Again, Reist did not respond.

"Jacob Ammann said to keep quiet, to not scold, nor abuse. Once the Amish saw their mistake, they did make another attempt, and on January 7, 1700, nine leaders confessed, ". . . that in this controversy and strict ban which we have practiced against you in Switzerland, we have gone far astray. We . . . acknowledge that we are deservedly excommunicated; therefore, stand blameworthy outside the church and desire to be reconciled to God and man as much as posible . . . and we therefore sincerely request . . . that you forbear with us and . . . forgive as much as you can forgive."

"In other words," said Jan, "five years later, Ammann's people saw their error and asked for forgiveness, but it was too late, according to Reist."

"Maybe Reist did not appreciate Ammann's attitude earlier. For instance, Ammann had written a paper which was sent to all the congregations about the steps he had taken according to Matthew 18."

Hans sighed. "There were ten times in that letter that repeated either 'I' or 'me' as Jacob Ammann. It was not written as most Anabaptists would write or speak.

"Perhaps it would have helped if they had attempted to reconcile earlier, because five years is a long time when you feel you have been mistreated and each had gone separate ways. It appears as if Hans Reist had been so hurt by the way that the matter was handled that he did not realize that Jacob Ammann and his group had some valid and important points. Foot washing was not a point of contention at the time. In the matter of dress, we too believe that our dress should be simple, not in pride and style and fashion. So far our people have been so poor it was never an important issue.

"It was quite an eye-opener to us when we reached Holland, and I thought of Jacob Ammann living here at one time. Don't misunderstand me. The Holland Mennonites have helped the suffering Brethren and they helped us very much. We praise and thank God for it. But most of them are rich.

"We have an example in Abraham who had great wealth yet kept his faith in God; and that he did not move to the city and build himself a palace. He lived in a tent, the only practical way to live with grazing animals on their land. His riches did not change Abraham. In our climate, that is not possible to live as he lived."

"However, we feel that we should dress and live so simply that the poor need not envy us. In Holland, the dress of wealthy young adults . . ." he shook his head. "Well, Jacob Ammann and his people might be wise to have a code of dress because once people are no longer poor, they won't wear such things as blue silk coats like our silk merchants wear when the poor hardly have enough clothes to keep warm or enough food to eat and some don't even have a roof over their heads."

Jan nodded. "I see your point."

Father said, "Yes, and sometimes I wonder how many generations will the Dutch Mennonites be rich and also keep the faith? I see more of a need to live on the land or else keep a simple trade. If the time should come when our people are no longer poor, we should teach our children to help others more, rather than showing our wealth; that heaven is our goal, not material possessions."

Jan agreed, and asked, "How do you feel about Jacob Ammann's practice of avoidance?"

Father stroked his beard a few times and said, "The ban has its place and there's times it is needful. There is an admonition in the scriptures 'with such a one not to eat.'"

Jan said, "That's in I Corinthians 5:11. When I first heard about this conflict, I studied that chapter, and yes, those words are there. But verse eight says, 'Therefore let us keep the feast not with the old leaven neither with the leaven of malice and wickedness, but with the unleavened bread of sincerity and truth.' That verse clearly speaks about communion and must be taken in context."

Father nodded. "I believe the lesson we can learn from both these splits is that situations like this too often reach the point that it brings out unchristian conduct and words which turn away 'babes in Christ.' At least Ammann's people, after they realized they were out of place, **repented**, **apologized**, and asked for **forgiveness**. It is not easy to reach this point—it is far easier to be too proud to admit a mistake causing the wounds to be too deep to heal.

"Both had their own interpretation of these scriptures. Only time will tell. 'Except the Lord bless the house, they labor in vain that build it.' As you said, it seems to me that this Keith split left a lot of wounds, yet hasn't resulted in another group that is following what the split was based on."

Jan just sighed and shook his head. His followers are scattered. "It seems to me that Keith and Ammann were both very zealous men and wanted to do what was right, but in time this zeal almost ran away with them."

Father nodded and replied, "Yes, zeal is like so many other things in life; it is a good servant, but a poor master. Reist and his followers felt the ban should be practiced for sinners. Then Ammann put them in the ban because they did not agree on a certain point, yet kept all the rest. Then they put Ammann in the ban. These disagreements were a poor light to the authorities and were used against us all. But there is also the example of Jesus whom the Pharisees accused of eating with sinners.

"I am afraid we need to be careful that we don't have the attitude of the Pharisees rather than the attitude of love that Jesus showed."

Jan nodded his agreement. "What you are telling me seems to show that it is not that Jacob Ammann did not have some valid arguments. It was more the way the matter was handled that caused the ill feelings or bitter feelings."

Father added as he cleared his throat, "Yes, and those bitter feelings on both sides are not in accord with God's words. Maybe in time healing will come. But I see another thing that is just as bad as the bitterness, and that is one side feeling they are spiritually superior to the other side. I believe both sides have been guilty of this."

Jan said, "Sadly, it was that way in the Quaker split, too.

Father nodded, "Yes, zeal, like so many other things is a good servant but a poor master."

CHAPTER ELEVEN

Anna and Mother kept glancing out the window as they sat at their spinning wheels. Christmas and New Year's had passed and several changes had occurred.

Jan Lensen had helped set up Mommy Rittenhouse's old loom in the little stone house. It needed a few new parts, but not many. The little house was barely large enough and the door would only open part ways.

Hans, Frances, and the children had moved in with a family in Germantown where Hans got work with a potter. Anna smiled to herself as she remembered Hans' statement, "I found it's another one of those things that's not as easy as it looks."

Father had smiled and said, "Don't you know that that is a good sign of an expert craftsman? It looks easy when he does it."

Today was Monday and several of the men had come from Skippack and stayed overnight for the meeting this morning. She was glad that Henry and Martin Kolb were along to offer advice. The men had gathered to make some decisions about the new settlement at the Pequea.

But now dinner was waiting for awhile already and still Father and Christian hadn't come back. As Anna glanced out the window once more, Mother said, "In a multitude of counselors, there is safety."

Anna nodded, "Yes, I know. No one said they'd be home for dinner, you know. Maybe we should eat."

"Yes, I was thinking that too. There are so many plans to make. Where would we be without the help and advice of these Brethren?"

"Well, I am sure glad someone suggested that Father weave the tow cloth," said Mother. It can be used for shelter if needed and it's the easiest way to put things in bags for pack horses. We surely didn't bring many bags along. It will be some time until we have the time to make a loom and set it up again."

As they ate their dinner, Anna said, "You know, I keep wondering if little Hans found room some place for all his many sheep and cows?"

Mother smiled and replied, "Yes, these flat stones in front of the fireplace were just ideal. The hickory nuts were the sheep and the butternuts the cows and oxen and the black walnuts his horses." She chuckled. "I have to chuckle every time I think of how worried he was when his hands were turning black when he'd helped Father shell those walnuts."

"Yes, Frances says that since he had seen those black men in Philadelphia, he often asked about the slaves. Frances said he told her he couldn't sleep much that night, since he couldn't wash it off. He was afraid if he'd turn black he might have to be a slave too."

"Well that explains why he was so upset about it and it wasn't until Father showed him that his hands were black too and that that is why they used walnuts to dye things."

Anna looked out the window once more and returned to her spinning. The afternoon was half gone when at last the men returned.

"Did you have dinner?"

"Yes, Jan Lensen's wife soon saw it would get late and put out bread and cheese and some hard cider. But after our walk we could still eat a bite if you have something left."

"What took you so long?"

"Oh everything. First we had to sort all the good advice and offers of help and see which we can use now and which we'll be able to use later."

"Claus says that our big chest that we moved to the barn when we put the loom in here, can stay until they add on to their house. We cannot take it until there's a wagon road. Actually, I guess all the chests will need to stay for now until we can take wagons through."

Mother and Anna looked at each other and nodded. "Yes, I can see . . . but it's where we keep everything we have. Guess, we'll each just take a set of clothes to wear and a few clothes until fall at least and pack a bag that someone can bring along once we have a cabin or two built."

"The men will scout out more land and decide where and what each family gets as soon as the weather looks promising. Someone has a tent they can use while scouting. Then Jacob Taylor or his brother Isaac can survey it for us."

"Martin Kolb promised to give us some wheat and rye seed as soon as they harvest and flail it. They suggest that we not only plant Indian corn for the first winter but also buckwheat. Someone promised seed for that."

Mother took a deep breath, "So much being given, how can we ever repay them?"

"That's what we said and they told us we may in time need to repay it many times over when others settle around us," answered Father, "which puts us *deef in die shuld* (deeply in debt)."

"Someone said to be sure to have at least one wolf trap. We'll also work to purchase guns and powder this winter yet. Business is so good, almost every tradesman can use a good worker."

"Yes and the first cabin is to be for us," said Father. Anna and Christian exchanged glances and nodded and Anna breathed a sigh of relief.

Then we may need to provide shelter for some things for the others while they live in temporary shelters. They will plan temporary shelters such as Pastorius made the first year; half dug out with saplings for a roof top. We'll have to find long grass to make a sod roof because there is no rye straw available."

"We'll also need enough nails for at least our cabin. Then we can take iron and make nails for the rest or else wait a year and use thatch."

"When Jan Lensen talked of forty-five miles of trail to be turned into a wagon road in time, some said it would be sensible for some of them to work from the lower end at the Brandywine. That's really not that far away. If a whole group works together, they can chop quite a few trees down, and later get the stumps out. Then we can work on our end."

"It sounds like you did have a multitude of counselors," smiled Mother. "Did they say anything more about the Indians?"

"Only that if we can find a place where the Indians had lived a long time there would be more open space and less clearing to do where they had their fields."

"There are only three small Indian villages in the area now. Johann Bondeli said that 'The one near where the Pequea Creek flows into the Susquhanna River is where are Shawnee from the south live with Chief Opessah. A Frenchman by the name of Martin Chartier who is married to an Indian woman lives among them."

Then further up near the Susquhanna River there is a village of Conoys. Bondeli says Peter Bezaillion told him that quite a number of miles up the river there is another village of Conoy Indians."

"Who is Peter Bezaillion?"

"He's a French fur trader who has traveled the path from the Brandywine to the Susquehanna perhaps more than any other white man. He uses pack horses to bring his furs down the trails. There are two trails, one called the Great Minquas Path or the Conestoga Path and the other is Peter's Road, which was probably an Indain path too. Peter works with a French Huguenot couple by the name of Letort. James Letort and his wife Ann were driven from France by religious persecution in 1686. They were fur traders living along the Schuylkill River before moving out by the Susquehanna some years ago."

"You mean to tell me a white woman has been living near where we are going for several years already?" asked Anna, surprised.

Christian nodded. "Not only that but her husband is often gone leaving her in charge of the Indian trade with some French servants."

Anna took a very deep breath and sighed. "Here I've been a bit fearful…and this woman is often out there…alone." She nodded, "She must be mighty spunky and have a deep faith. I'll have to tell that to the rest of the women as soon as I see them at meeting. That's good news to us women."

"Yes and several of the men went to talk with surveyor Jacob Taylor. Did you know he only surveyed four thousand acres last fall?"

Later while they were eating super Father said, "Several also offered to go together to buy us traps or give some they don't have the time to use anymore since animals aren't so plentiful around Germantown anymore. They suggested we get some white oak strips ready to be made into baskets. But we should leave them in bundles because they are easier to carry on a pack horse. They won't take long to weave. Martin Mylin said his wife is making the fish nets. George Miller has started working for a wheelwright now and likes it."

"We'll need at least one two-man cross-cut saw to saw short lengths for shingles. I'm glad we brought ours. It was one of those items we weren't sure about."

"Then there was also the matter of the land. Some men were still afraid of losing their land because they were not English citizens. When we brought this up they did admit that there could be trouble about inheriting the land if you were not a naturalized citizen."

"Also they have a bill before the Assembly asking for the right to affirm for people who will not swear due to their conscience. They'll ask the assemblies for a bill for religious Societies to dispose of land in Pennsylvania."

"They also said that the best way of being sure of keeping our land was to pay for it as soon as possible."

Mother lifted her eyebrows, "Yes that would be nice, but of course, its impossible."

"Don't be too sure. They want to check around. Some of the first settlers and Quakers may have money we can borrow. They feel that if enough people can loan us a small amount we may be able to pay most of it. We aren't certain yet how much the price will be. There was some talk of the good soil going for a higher price, perhaps £500 for 10,000 acres."

"Well it's worth more, isn't it?"

"Yes, I'd rather pay more for good soil any day," nodded Father.

A few weeks later in February the bill was presented by the assembly. But Governor Gookin argued that long and bitter experience in England warned against giving religious communities any power to control lands when he found out about it.

"What we need," said Martin Kolb, "is something to show them we are harmless like our Dordrecht Confession of Faith in English."

"We have already gotten ready to send them notice that we want another printing of the Dordrecht Confession in German," answered Jacob Gottschalk. "To ask for a printing in English the same year might be too much."

"Why not ask for that next year then? It will take them awhile to get it translated anyway," suggested Martin Kolb. "We can be of great benefit to our own people by buying large tracts and letting others get them through us. Rather that than the land speculators who want to make a huge profit."

There was a general agreement to this and Jacob Gottschalk nodded too. "We can only try. It may help that we now have money to pay for it."

*   *   *

Several weeks later Christian took a deep breath as he watched the riders ahead of him with their bundles tied on back. One contained the tent. There were a few pots and pans for cooking and several bundles of apple trees they were hoping to plant. At long last they were on their way to scout out more land. The surveyor would meet with them two days later. They had started after dinner and expected to sleep near the Brandywine Creek and start off at daybreak for the forty-five-mile trek up to the Pequea Creek area. There was fresh bread and some cold meat in a basket plus some Indian corn meal. They expected to find some meat or fish to eat with it. Johann Bondeli was taking the lead.

That evening they scratched together a pile of dry oak leaves where they set up their tent with some furs and blankets to roll into. They slept with their coats on.

The next morning they did not bother cooking breakfast but ate bread and cold meat so as to start out as soon as it was light enough to see the trail. The trail was not hard to follow and a few places they saw horse tracks in wet spots although they weren't recent.

It does show this trail is being used, thought Christian as he mentally checked the trees on each side of the trail and counted in his mind how many would need chopped down in order to make a wagon road.

When it was nearing dinnertime, Martin Mylin rode ahead, and suddenly a shot rang out. By the time they caught up with him, he had a small fire going and was skinning a rabbit.

"How'd you get a fire going so soon?" asked Christian.

"Oh, I brought along a bunch of flax tow to pack my tools in," said Martin Mylin. "With the flint and steel I soon had some tow then twigs going. Just get that pot filled with water and we'll soon have a good dinner while the horses rest."

Just as Christian was stirring in the cornmeal one of the horses neighed shrilly. Soon an answer came back from up the trail. Most of the horses answered and now more returned the answer showing it was not a lone rider coming. All eyes turned when a string of loaded pack horses and a rider appeared.

"Peter Bezaillion!" yelled Johann Bondeli. The buckskin clad rider acknowledged the greeting and started talking in English.

When the man answered in German he nodded to show he understood it, but answered in English with a strong French accent.

"How did you know it was me?" he asked.

"We were told that Peter would bring a load of furs as soon as the weather turned nice," answered Bondeli.

"Will you share what we have in the pot?" asked Christian.

Peter nodded and Christian asked, "Would you by any chance have salt? It seems we forgot to bring salt."

"Yes, yes, I have ze salt," nodded Peter, as he opened his leather saddle bags and brought out a leather pouch of salt. His observant eye took in the rabbit skin and the bag of cornmeal.

"I'll trade some salt for ze rabbit skin," he offered. A linen handkerchief was offered to put the salt in and Peter took a strip of rawhide and tied it up.

"Now you are fixed," he said. His eyes quickly took in the shovels, the apple trees, and the tent.

"Where are you planning to settle? Where Taylor was surveying last fall?"

Martin Kendig nodded, "Maybe you can help us out? We asked Taylor to survey 10,000 acres of land near the head of the Pequea. In late October he surveyed 4,000 acres of land there, but we have been told that if we can find land that had Indian villages and Indian fields years ago there would be more open land with less clearing to do."

Peter Bezaillion nodded. "Yes! True! But ze land at ze head of ze Pequea . . . he shrugged . . . if you go on back ze trail a mile or more and more southwest where ze land is level where it has springs. Indians always chose land that was level if they could for their fields," he said, "and land that had springs. There is a big spring in there somewhere. Ze Indians would probably have a village near ze Big Spring."

"Do you bring all your furs down this trail by pack horse?" asked young John Miller.

Peter nodded, "Ze only way. You make a wagon road?" he asked with arched eyebrows.

"We are planning to," said Hans. "Can you teach us some Indian sign language?"

He nodded. "Better yet . . . I can teach you ze Indian language. Maybe," said Peter, "you make ze road and we help chop trees. You get ze wagon," he pointed, "and pack horses, and we pay you to haul our furs. Good for you," he pointed at young John.

"Good for me," he pointed to himself.

"Me a trader," he laughed. "Most trade with Indians in these parts. Letorts keep trading post on Susquahanna. Indians bring furs by canoe."

Christian asked, "My wife thinks this Ann Letort must be a brave woman with a strong faith to keep the trading post."

"Yes, yes, yes! Ann a woman in a thousand. She all alone with French servants when Jacques go back to England or west to meet Indians. Not willing to become a Catholic, rather flee France when Louis, XV, says 'Convert or die.'

"Yes, she brave woman. Many men afraid of whiskey traders. Not Ann, ze whiskey traders they come and give ze Indians whiskey for furs and cheat ze Indians. Then young Indian braves cold, no blankets, no nothing . . . just angry, even maybe dangerous.

"But Ann she give ze Indians credit, you pay me when bring furs and Ann she give the Indians fair trade. She give good things and right at her door step come ze whiskey traders.

"Yes, yes," nodded Peter.

"Ze English and ze Swede Polly Carpus Rose and Thomas Jenner. They come and try and get ze furs for whiskey.

"Ann she get ze leather bull whip . . .," he raised his arm to show how she used the bullwhip, "and she whip ze whiskey traders till she drive them away. Happen back in 1693 or so. But ze whiskey traders they try and get even. In February of 1694, Ann had to appear before the Governor and ze council to answer their charges. But this time Ann not alone, Captain Jacques Letort he come home. When he go to England, he was captured by French war ship and put in prison and almost on gallows." He shook his head and showed a rope at his throat. "Take him two years to come home. But he came with the right papers to be fur trader for big London Company."

"What happened in court?" asked Hans.

"Oh, ze Swede he try and say she want French to conquer English because she French. They blame her for contacts with strange Indians. And yes, Ann say strange Indians whose language she no understand came to house. They say she whip and call names. And yes she say she whip them for bringing whiskey and in her anger may have called them names," he chuckled. "Ze governor and Council they dismissed all charges," he snapped his fingers. "Know other men just want fur trade. Fur trade bring big battles. Indian chiefs complain to William Penn of whiskey traders. Penn say to Indian 'Chiefs, make laws to stop this.' Ann help Penn make laws work," he chuckled as he rubbed his hands in satisfaction. As he rose to move on he said, "Maybe once you settle I bring my wife Martha to meet your wife."

Most of the men were chuckling as they watched the string of pack horses go down the trail.

"Won't that be a story to tell the women," chortled Hans as they mounted their horses and headed up the trail. It was late afternoon by the time they reached the winding Pequea Creek area.

They rode a mile or more.

"Peter Bezaillion said southwest of here." They tied their horses and looked around. "Let's spread out as far as we can and still stay in sight of each other and walk southwest and see what we find."

They walked over quite a bit of land and liked what they saw. There were quite a few open meadows and springs. The sun was setting as they found the Big Spring. It was beautiful. There was a general agreement that, yes, near here would have been a good place for an Indian village.

Martin Kendig looked around. "Here would be a good place to plant the apple trees."

"It would be easy to water them this summer if it gets dry," nodded Hans.

"Let's walk around a little more to the north and see if we can't make a full circle. I'd say we came about three-fourth of a circle," said Martin Kendig, as he squinted at the sun.

They tried it and before long were back at the Pequea Creek. After that they soon found their horses.

Martin Mylin once more started a fire and they took the fish seine they brought along and before long came back with several fish which they cleaned for supper. The horses were once more led to the creek to drink and ate some of the long grass from last year.

The tent was set up not far from the fire, with wood ready to add during the night so they wouldn't have to start a fresh fire in the morning.

"If we'd have used our heads we'd have taken the gun along this afternoon and got that Indian hen we saw or some of the squirrels."

"Why waste powder when we have good fish here for the taking?" asked George Miller.

There was a general nodding of agreement. "Those fish were good, although they wouldn't have been near as good without the salt. I'm surprised Peter Bezaillion wanted that rabbit skin."

"I thought rabbit skin wasn't worth anything much?" said Hans.

Bondeli chuckled, "Peter Bezaillion must have been smart enough to stay ahead of all the other traders and keep on the good side of the Indians too. He was smart enough not to offer to just give us the salt. We'd have said, 'no, no we don't want to take your salt.' But when he offered a trade . . . " Again there was a nodding of heads.

"Peter Bezaillion and Martin Chartier, I've heard say," said Bondeli, "are among only a small number of white men who have explored the lands and large rivers many hundreds of miles west of here. They say they explored a mighty river called the Mississippi from Canada all the way for many hundreds of miles to where it enters the ocean. I don't know if these are just rumors or not, but they do have contacts with western Indians. I've heard they are rather close-mouthed about what they know."

"Why, if they are French, have they come to an English country to live?" asked Christian. "Why did they leave Canada?"

Bondeli took a deep breath, "Because they were paid very little by the French, I've heard. Here, they can do well, like this Ann Letort who was driving away the whiskey traders with a bullwhip."

"It's not nonresistance as we've been taught, is it?" asked young John Miller.

Christian snapped back, "Giving whiskey to the Indians until they are drunk so you can rob them of a years work. Just how much difference is there between that and what Christ did in the temple with the money changers?"

George Miller nodded, "And how much difference is there between using a bullwhip and leather thongs which Christ used?"

Again there was a murmer of agreement as the men prepared for sleep.

The next morning, Martin Kendig suggested, "Let's go a bit above this spring and make a straight line westward for about two miles or so. I'll go first, then Martin Mylin, Christian, Hans, and Wendell Bauman. Then Jacob, John Miller, and John Funk you walk the other way a mile or so. Try and pace your steps to about three feet. Nine hundred steps is roughly a bit over one-half mile. Then we'll all walk due south for one or one and a half miles. So walk down one side of where you started and up about a good distance from there. Try to find a spring or a creek on each of your areas. The great Conestoga Trail is running through all of this the way it looks. Take your small axes along and mark a few trees to show where you've been and if you find an area you like and feel you want, step it off roughly and mark it with your knife in some trees. We'll use the Roman Numerals. I'll take 'I' and so on up to 'VIII' for John Funk. Where you start, make your mark and go to the next tree to stop. If Isaac or Jacob Taylor come they'll likely be on the trail. Where you cross the trail put three stones in a pile so they'll see them if they should come before noon. We'll meet back here at noon and whoever comes first can start some fish and porridge. Any questions or suggestions?"

"Why not send the fish seine along with young John?" suggested Hans.

"Good idea!" nodded Martin as they started out. "Christian you start here," said Martin as he slashed a mark in the tree. Martin Mylin and Martin Kendig went on counting their steps as they went.

Christian took his bearings. The moss was on the north side of the trees. To go due south he'd have to keep facing the moss. He followed an old trick he'd learned from Father. For every one hundred steps put a pebble in your pocket.

All the way down he found no spring, but at the bottom as he crossed over he found a nice small run flowing south that he expected came from a spring. He followed the run and it took a big turn east but then ran northwest again, yes this was pleasing to him. Again, he went back to where he had first found the run counting his steps till he wanted to turn north. Here he put several stones and headed north a mile and a half. Near the upper end he found another spring and soon another run flowing north this time instead of south. He went up and hunted east to where he had started. Soon he crossed a small run; yes, this was pleasing. He started down a few hundred feet and crossed over again looking for the source of the spring and run. Soon he found them. There was not just one spring but two feeding the run. Christian looked at the sun. Yes, there were more open spaces and meadow in the area of the springs and some swampy areas too. He stopped as a wild goose hissed at him trying to protect a nest of eggs.

"Yes, hatch them out and grow them big and fat," he told her. "We need more feather bed covers for the winter."

As he returned to where he had started to find his "III" mark on a large oak tree, he almost stepped on a spotted fawn hidden in a nest of leaves. It was beautiful and so tiny.

As he headed back down again, he marked more trees, and at one point picked up a reddish brown rock. It was a sandstone, not the gray limestone. Sandstone was easier to quarry he'd heard. Already he thought of Anna's wish for a stone house like the tiny Rittenhouse homestead. Not now, of course, but some day in the future. You can always dream about it they'd said at Skippack. As he returned south once more, the stones soon changed back to limestone again.

It was close to noon when he headed back to the spring. The surveyors had just arrived, and Hans and Martin Kendig were talking with them.

"How many acres do you want?" asked Isaac Taylor.

"I want 500 acres just west of here, to start at the run that flows over to where Wendell Bauman has his staked out."

"But, but, I had planned to go above the other track," said Isaac scratching his head, "where we had planned last fall near the head-waters of the Pequea."

Martin Kendig nodded, "We hadn't explored this section last fall. We find this area more to our liking so we want you to survey this." Isaac wrote down 'Hans Herr, 500 acres.'

"My area is marked with a V," said Hans. "I went a bit more east than we'd planned on in order to include the run I told you about."

"I'll take the extra strip if it gives one," said Martin Kendig.

"I'll take 500 acres due west of here," said Christian.

"I only want 250 acres since I plan to operate a blacksmith shop," said Martin Mylin. "My mark is a II."

"I'll take 500 acres west of that," said Martin Kendig. "My mark is a I. In fact, once the rest have all they want you can put the rest in my name. I'll be buying for some others."

The smell of fresh fish was inviting and soon they were eating fresh catfish.

After dinner which Isaac shared with them, Wendell Bauman put in his bid for 500 acres too and Jacob Miller said, "My son and I each want about 500 acres. You can put it all in one tract in my name."

"We explored further up from where we were last fall," said Wendell Bauman. "I'd like my tract to extend up into that tract about a third of a mile or so, then not as wide to include that spring that's on there. In other words only about a half mile wide and more like two miles long."

Isaac shook his head, "You people are asking for a lot of extra work here."

"Yes," nodded Martin Kendig, "we understand that. We're willing to pay extra to get what we want."

Then there's John Funk. "Five hundred for you too?" he asked. John nodded.

"I suppose you realize," Isaac said, "that Penn always adds about six percent extra for roads later on." They nodded.

They talked among themselves awhile and then walked the length and breadth of the large plot together or around the square as each mark was found.

"I'll start with Wendell Bauman's tract and work west from there," said Isaac Taylor.

Soon it was planned that Martin Kendig would stay and work with the surveyor while the rest would return to Germantown.

CHAPTER TWELVE

It was a pleasant sunny day in *brach monat* (June) and Christian and John Miller, sons of George, had gone to the Pequea to fish.

As they headed back over the Indian trail, they were surprised to see a number of horses and riders appearing. As they stepped back off the trail, they were amazed to see some of the finest horses they had ever seen with well-dressed people riding them.

"I'm going to follow them and see where they go," whispered John as he handed his fish to Christian.

"Be careful," Christian whispered as he debated if he should follow also, but then no one would know what became of them. They had to be important people! Young John had taken to the woods, and hunting like a duck to water. More than likely they were going to the Indian village and John wouldn't get lost.

Christian went back to the big spring with his fish. The women cleaned them and put them in cold water until dinnertime. When the men came for dinner, there was a lot of excitement.

"That was Governor Gookin you saw," said Martin Kendig after Christian had told his story.

We met them further down the trail and asked one of the last riders. He said it was Governor Gookin and there are several chiefs here from the Five Nations of Iroquois from New York who are the rulers of the Indians here.

A while later young John Miller returned. He was rather out of breath but said, "They stopped to water the horses and I'd heard what they told Martin Kendig, who it was and all. I talked to the same man and I asked who the interpreter was. I thought it might be Peter Bezaillion, but he said no it would be Martin Chartier this time from the Shawnee village at the mouth of the Pequea."

About ten days later, Martin Kendig took the gray mare the settlers had bought together and left for Philadelphia hoping to get their land purchase finalized. They had a short meeting that evening before he left as all listened to Father's prayer, as he put it into God's hands and said, "Not our will but thine be done."

Christian thought once again of the extra work they'd asked the surveyor to do. Martin Kendig had stayed there with Isaac Taylor and had then asked him to go farther west to the tract he had and not as far south for his tract and most of Martin Mylin's tract. It was on this farthest west of the tracts that Martin Kendig had built his dugout where they and the Martin Mylins planned to live.

There were anxious days until he returned. Everyone's mind seemed to be on Martin, and many were the prayers raised on his behalf.

When he returned five days later, he said that Penn had plans to settle more people further southwest near branches of the Potomac. The Indians strongly advised against settlements in that area as a war was dragging between the Tuscaroras to the south and the Five Nations. But Gookin told them that Penn would be sending them several wampum belts about a matter close to their homes.

Penn was "requiring their friendship" to the group of Palatines who had settled less than five miles away. The Indians were extremely pleased to hear from good friend William Penn and said that the new neighbors were safely seated at their new location.

Gookin also talked to the Shawnees from the mouth of the Pequea. Chief Opessah was losing his hold over the younger war-like braves and some were leaving and following Chartier as their chief.

"You mean William Penn sent a special message to the Indians on our behalf and sent the Governor to bring them the message?" wondered Father in awe.

Martin nodded, "He will send them wampum belts, too. For so long our people have been punished, jailed, put to death, and taxed until poor for the sake of our faith . . . and now . . . are we worthy of this, this special friendship and protection? May God bless Penn if not now, then in the world to come."

"Yes, it sure seems Penn has had more than his share of troubles," agreed Father. "New ideas may be like two rivers running together. It will give some turbulence until they flow smoothly again."

"You mean a little like the church at Germantown? The many people from many places had different ideas," said Christian, "and not just the congregation, but the people of Germantown did too."

Father nodded, "Yes, we need to work together here or we'll run into the same problems. We saw it when we first moved to the Palatinate. It was new uncharted ground for us in a sense. The burned-out buildings and overgrown fields were not so different in a sense than what we have here. It took a lot of yielding and working together. In fact, that is why I feel it is best if we all move to this side of Pequea Creek. This way we can all help each other better and won't leave one or two families stranded on the other side when the creek is higher. When more families arrive, then we can expand; but for now we need each others' help and fellowship," said Father, and the rest nodded in agreement.

It was Sunday evening in the middle of hay month (July) and the evening meal together was over. They had made it a practice to gather together on Sunday evenings. In fact they practically lived outside under the trees when it was warm and in the grass in the new apple orchard when it was cooler.

A log cabin had been built for Father and Mother, Christian and Anna and their new baby whom they had named John, the English form of Hans, since there was already Old Hans, young Hans, and little Hans. Yes, Christian and Anna were blessed with their first son!

Also, in that same cabin, Jacob Miller's son Samuel had been born on June 22, 1711. They had moved in for now too and Father and Mother had moved out to the shelter.

All the extra clothes and tools for the other settlers were stored in the cabin. When it rained some went to the cabin and some to Martin Kendig's dugout. They had made a few rough three-sided log shelters that would be used later for cattle and had finally decided to wait till the next year to build most of the log cabins when they would have rye straw for thatch roofs. The women said they would rather spend the money for windows than for iron to make nails. So any spare time was spent on making shingles and nails this year, while windows would come next year, Lord willing. Clearing land and getting it ready to plant was the main priority though.

Christian looked across the field to the flax that was growing so tall. This morning it had been a breathtaking sea of blue that was about the brightest blue you ever saw in the sky. In the afternoon sun, the blue flowers had closed, only to be a fresh blue again in the morning. The Indian corn was about waist high and the Indian squash and pumpkins among the corn had golden blossoms. The small plot of oats was in head. They looked so good as did the gardens. Soon it would be time to plant the first fall turnips.

Christian thought back to those hectic first days and weeks of moving, decision making, and building, and the many little irritations and adjustments. He sighed as he thought of the times there had been conflicting opinions of what was best to do. And how often it was Father or even Mother who had had the wisdom to make a compromise or do some of each so that peace was kept.

Once Mother had said, "We always put our winter food at more than one place." Plus Mother and Father had lived through this before when they moved to the destroyed and burned-out Palatinate where many people lived together in close quarters. They knew a little of how to make things easier for others.

Now tonight as dusk approached everyone just sat quietly thinking their own thoughts. Christian held out his arms as Anna came carrying baby John. They wanted to enjoy nature's spectacular show together.

"You know," said Anna, "I miss the storks and the other birds we had at home. And they were right," she chuckled, "that the first time we smelled a skunk we knew what it was without seeing it. But nothing prepared me for the beauty of the fireflies. I had no idea God's creation had anything like this," she said, as she watched the first ones light up in the gathering dusk.

"Yes," nodded Christian, "see how they come out of the grass and other vegetation. First they are close to the ground then gradually they fly higher. It is beautiful. There is so much to be thankful for."

"Yes," Anna nodded, "I don't know yet what the winter will be like, but I was a bit afraid."

"Afraid of what?"

"Well, I . . . everything I suppose. For the baby . . . the winter . . . the wolves . . . bears . . . and wild cats! And so far I haven't seen any of them yet. But now that we're all adjusted and are living almost like the Indians," she stopped as Christian laughed, "well aren't we?"

He nodded, "Yes, I guess we are fairly close. I just hadn't looked at it that way. But yes, we're living a lot nearer like the Indians, then we are as the ones back home in so many ways. We're even eating corn porridge instead of bread."

"Well now it seems so beautiful and peaceful. The beauty of the wild flowers and the big trees hundreds of years old. The fireflies seem so beautiful. Something extra special. Every time I see them I have to think of little Hans and the awe in his voice when he asked his Mother where they came from. When Frances told him God had made them he breathlessly asked, 'Are they all God's little lights?'"

"Yes," nodded Christian, "and the spring peepers and now the frogs too. It makes me think of the verse, 'The earth is the Lord's and the fullness there of.'"

"Somehow," said Anna, "my fears have faded . . . it's, well . . . the perscution our people have endured for many generations . . . we were used to that and trusted God would make a way for us. But here . . . this was new . . . we didn't like going out in the dark at a strange place . . . the things we're used to . . . it's like at home in the dark, you sort of know your way even if it is dark." She took a deep breath, "But now that I've found so much beauty here . . . it brings a peace . . . yes, man has always had troubles and problems and I suppose always will. We must just learn anew that God's help and strength will be given in the trials if we don't let our fears cast a dark shadow over everything we have and look at," she sighed.

"You mean like being thankful for Indian porridge instead of being so hungry for bread you can hardly eat it?" asked Christian.

Anna nodded, "Or seeing a big black bear or a wild cat behind every big tree when you go into the woods."

Christian threw back his head and laughed, "And it took the tiny firefly to take care of the bears!" They chuckled.

Eventually everyone drifted to their shelters and beds. Tomorrow there would again be a lot of work to do and the men wanted to work at daylight. Then in the heat, such as they hadn't quite been used to at home, they would make baskets or do some debarking or some other such activity.

Breakfast usually was wild raspberries and corn porridge and milk. Oh how good the milk was again now that they had some fresh cows after doing without for awhile. Hans had located a bee tree and George Miller's son another one. Father had made a hive out of a hollow tree and when they'd seen a swarm they had taken all the pots and pans and banged them with metal ladles and spoons and now they had a swarm of their own.

Martin Kendig had said, "The Bible talks of a land of milk and honey. Now that we have cows and bees; we'll soon have a land of milk and honey too."

Father was getting more hives ready. If they didn't see any more swarms, at least they'd be ready for the winter when you could move them out of the bee trees by making a cut above the tree with a saw and one below chopping out a portion with an axe.

There were quite a few strings of beans drying in the shelters and more were growing. They were eating some small red beets from the first planting. It was an adjustment to do without bread as that had been a staple of life. When people had collected food for them few had extra wheat. The wheat was the chief money crop bringing one *franc* and eight *groshen* ($1.00 and 16¢). In fact, a bushel of wheat took about three days of work to pay for and they'd kept only as much as was needed for their own use. But extra Indian corn was fed to cattle, chickens, and geese. So they had gathered most of what had been given and had it ground at the Brandywine Mill. The rest had been kept for planting.

But now the buckwheat was starting to bloom. That would be a change from the corn when it was ready and the huckleberries were starting to turn color too. There were plans made to dry some of those for the winter too.

*   *   *

About a month later on a Saturday evening there were shouts of joy as Martin Kolb and Gerhart Clemens came with a string of pack horses loaded with bags of wheat and rye.

Oh, what rejoicing they brought. How good to see these Brethren after all these months. And to think of Sunday and hearing a sermon as well . . . it gave wings to the spirit, thought Christian, as he greeted the Brethren. They had not seen these men since they had helped build their cabin. As Anna came out, Gerhart Clemens said, "My wife sent something special along for you," as he opened his saddle bags and took out a small brown jug.

"What's in it?" asked Anna.

"Yeast starter!"

Anna raised her hands in surprise, "Oh! Yeast! Wonderful!"

"Yes, here's a little bag of flour to go with it," he said as he lifted a bag out of the other saddle bag.

"Oh, if tomorrow wasn't Sunday, I'd start some bread tomorrow morning."

"I believe Martin has two loaves along for tomorrow. But Ann said, 'Get this in a cold spring as soon as possible so it wont spoil.' So I had it in one overnight."

Anna nodded and went to the spring not far from the cabin with the jug. How good of Ann to think of them like this.

Martin Kolb came carrying a bag too. "Wilhelmina Rittenhouse sent this along too. For you or whoever needs it," he said.

Anna took the bag inside and opened it. "Oh!" she exclaimed as she saw what a treasure she'd been sent. From the rags they got for paper making, she'd cut out the least worn parts of clothing, which was just what one needed for baby and children's clothes. They were so much softer. A whole bag full and buttons and hooks and eyes yet, too.

"God bless you, Wilhelmina," said Anna to herself as she thought, "I feel rich, a whole bag of soft clothes to share with all the Mothers of little ones and enough hooks and eyes and buttons to last us for several years. A sermon to anticipate. Flour and yeast to bake bread and huckleberries and blackberries, too. Cabbage and beans and lots of onions braided into strings are hanging under the porch roof. And better yet, there will be bread for all tomorrow."

The precious wheat and rye bags were stacked in the bedroom until planting time. The men left to walk through some of the fields ready to plant to see which ones needed the stumps and roots removed yet. They stayed to help most of the week. It was a wonderful help to use their horses to work the soil. They only had one harness but Anna heard them plan how they could improvise another one.

On Monday morning, Anna sang as she kneaded her bread dough. She sang many of the same songs that were sung yesterday after a gentle rain had begun to fall and they had gathered inside. It seemed there was new life and spirit in everyone's heart. And Martin's thought-provoking sermon had also refreshed their hearts. Today there was a fresh resolve in Anna's heart to be less selfish and more yielding. As she greased her Dutch Oven with goose fat before putting her round loaf of dough in the pan, she was debating if she should share this with all the rest of the families. They'd all had bread and butter yesterday for the first time in months. But this one loaf would hardly be enough to share with everyone.

Carefully she placed it in the pot in a bed of red embers she'd prepared and placed red embers over the lid too. Maybe she could just share with Mother and Father and Hans and Frances since the George Millers had moved back to their own shelter now that their baby was older.

She waited until the bread was a nice light brown before lifting the pot off the embers. The hot pot would bake awhile longer. She got some beans and beets ready for dinner and just as she was lifting the golden round loaf out of the pot she heard someone sniff behind her.

"Yes, doesn't it smell good," said Anna as she turned around to show Christian her beautiful loaf of bread. Anna gasped in surprise to find an Indian standing there! She dropped her loaf of bread as she froze and stood there open-mouthed.

Quickly the Indian picked up the bread, grunted, nodded, and went out the door and down the path.

Numbly Anna watched his bare back until he was out of sight. She took a deep breath . . . Well I wanted to share it . . . but this wasn't exactly what I had in mind. Here she'd never yet met an Indian face to face . . . yes, the ones at Skippack had said they walk quietly so you don't realize they are there; but it all happened so fast she told Christian when he came for dinner. The smell of fresh bread was still in the cabin but the bread was gone. Father and Mother also heard all about it when they returned with their huckleberries.

Father just looked at Anna's bare feet and smiled. "I wonder if he saw what size your feet were. Didn't you say that at Skippack they brought a pair of moccasins for some bread and you said you got some worn-out ones for the pattern. Now maybe you won't have to make some," he laughed.

Gerhart Clemens and Martin Kolb found it amusing too when they heard Anna's tale and said she might have to wait a little till the moccasins were ready.

But the next morning Anna watched in open-mouthed wonder as the Indian came and he and Christian talked in sign language and he lifted a skin from his shoulder and laid it on the ground. Out he poured peaches. Anna's mouth watered just looking at them as she remembered the ones they had on the ship. Peaches! He'd brought them peaches!

She watched as he and Christian made signs and spoke a few words.

Then Christian walked toward the cabin as Anna came to the door. Christian said, "I'm going with him. Seems they have extra peaches we can pick and apparently he gave Queen Conquegas some bread and she sent him to tell us we can have them if we want them."

When Christian returned nearly at suppertime, he told everyone, "The Indian's name is Shahaise. He was along with his people when William Penn made the treaty with the Indians and met Penn. You sure can tell that he thinks a lot of Penn. He also had all the peaches he could carry. In fact, there are quite a lot there. We can dry them for winter just like we did the apples. We'll all go tomorrow and take the horses and bags."

"All?"

"Well, all the men, I meant. You can get a fire ready; then once it's only embers you slice them and can string them like you do the beans and hang them above the embers till they are partly dry and finish them later in the sun, can't you?"

Mother nodded and said, "I believe we should borrow another black pot with a lid and bake the rest of that flour into bread to take along to Conquegas."

Anna nodded, "I had been so happy about the bread and wished to share with everyone . . . but it wasn't enough and now if everyone got peaches instead . . . and enough to dry yet too . . . it's more than I could have dreamed."

Mother nodded, "If the bread can help make friends with the Indians, Ann Clemens will have given a priceless gift. Far beyond a little flour and yeast. When we give our own few fish and loaves we never know what blessing may come from it.

Anna thought *later maybe it's good I was too shocked to pick up the bread myself. Thank you Lord.*

CHAPTER THIRTEEN

Christian sighed once more as he dipped the linen rag in the warm comfrey water and put it on the cut on his knee. He shook his head. To do something so foolish like this right at wheat harvest time! Yet it was as Anna had said, "Better a cut than a copperhead bite." He still wasn't exactly sure how he'd manage to cut himself with the sickle while trying to kill that copperhead snake that he'd found at the edge of the wheat field.

Everyone else was out in the wheat field; even Mother had gone along too. She said she'd cut wheat awhile, and then care for the children. Today they were cutting in his field. Yesterday they'd cut in Hans' field.

His thoughts went back to the Palatinate as he thought of the Amish split. They had tried in 1711 to reconcile with the Swiss Brethren, but there was no response.

Then he thought of the other situation that took place in 1711. What a shock it had been for everyone to learn that the Tuscarora Indians had wiped out the settlement at New Bern in Carolina; the place where they had at first planned to settle before William Penn's offer had looked so much better. Had that been God's guidance? At least 70 to 100 settlers had been killed. Nothing had been heard since of the Mennonite Nussbaum family.

Mennonite Jacob Wismer had managed to survive by giving an Indian a few leaves of tobacco and then ran for his life. Christian had heard he'd run ninety miles that first day. "Not impossible if fear was pushing you," said Christian to himself. Reports were he'd settled in Bucks County, Pennsylvania, now.

It was also in the fall of 1711 that Johann Anton Weber had moved from Germantown with his three sons Henry, Jacob, and George. They had rented land from the Bondeli tract and later built a steep-roofed one and one-half story cabin with squared-off dove-tailed logs.

Christian smiled to himself as he pondered how the plans had changed for most of them. They had done so well with the furs that first winter, that they'd bought iron and made nails and put on wood shingled roofs on most of the cabins. Wendell Bauman had built a full two-story log cabin with dove-tailed corners. Most of the rest had worked on their logs over winter and had made dove-tailed corners too. In fact, Martin Kendig had chosen to build his cabin of all walnut logs.

Many of them had built arch cellars under their cabins for the storage of food in summer and root crops during the winter months.

Mother and Anna hadn't been satisfied with the hole underneath the floor of the cabin and last year they had chosen the highest point of land on their tract to build a small arch cellar with a vent in the roof. First they had worked at digging out the hole, then they had put in the walls and steps leading down to it. Then they split wide boards and propped them up in the form of an arch-shaped roof. They gathered the brownish sandstones that were round or squarish and had split long gray limestones to put between the sandstones to make a strong arch.

They put the mortar on the boards first, then a row of the brown sandstone squares followed by long thin pieces of limestone between each row. They'd put a vent in the roof so there would be circulation when the door opened, and the air wouldn't get stale, and then covered it with the soil again.

Mother and Anna had dreams of building a brown stone house there some day. It was south of the Conestoga Road and they would have to dig a well, but, it sure was a nice setting.

Christopher Francis, who was a Reformed Church member from Switzerland, and was known as an extremely strong man, had settled on the tract above George Miller.

In 1712, Martin Kendig had sold 2,000 acres to the French Huguenot family of Mary Ferree and her son-in-law, Isaac LeFevre, who had come over by way of New York. Mary Ferree had lived in Strasbourg in Alsace and soon the whole area was called New Strasbourg, or Neu Strasbourg. Isaac LeFevre's family had all been martyred. The story was told of how they'd once hidden their Bible by baking it into a loaf of bread.

As Christian put more wood on the fire and stirred the rabbit that was cooking for dinner, he thought back over the four years they lived here. They had their fill of Indian corn that first year. Without it, they'd have gone hungry many times. That first winter had been rather hard at times and trying to keep warm was the hardest for most, but, game had been plentiful. What a thrill it had been the first time he'd seen an elk with its wide-spread and immense antlers. He had looked so stately and majestic that it was almost a shame to shoot him. They'd cured the legs with salt and smoked them and had made many a meal from it; but, they'd run out of salt that summer of 1712, and as soon as the first wheat crop was ready to thresh out they'd threshed three bushels and Martin Kendig had put it on the old gray mare and taken it to the mill. He'd gotten one bushel of salt for their three bushels of wheat and it had been carefully divided among them. The first wheat crop had brought them more money for powder and shot for a year and windows for all the cabins plus a supply of salt, and most had made payments on their land. In fact, Hans had paid his land in March 1713.

Martin Kendig had returned to Philadelphia on October 17, 1713, and had paid his first quit rent. Quit rent had been established by William Penn as a sort of tax or source of income at one-fourth cent an acre. The trouble was that most land owners did not bother paying it and then Penn did not get the income he had been expecting. By now, Penn had had several strokes and his second wife, Hannah Penn, was managing his affairs and seemed to be doing well.

Then, just before New Year's last winter on December 30, 1714, Martin Kendig, he, and Hans had gone to Philadelphia and paid a year's quit rent when they'd taken flour down and brought supplies back.

With the help of many others, last year had marked the opening of the wagon road called the Conestoga Road. James Logan had financed a wagon and horses which young John Miller drove most times. At last they had been able to bring home the chests that had stayed with friends at Germantown for so long, and also purchased more pottery. They had managed to make some larger crocks from the local clay, but most of their smaller pieces had not turned out the best. Neither did anyone seem to have the interest to become a pottery maker.

Father had finally bought the old Rittenhouse loom, and John Miller brought it home on his wagon. They'd sure been glad for the bags they'd brought along, and also made most of the tow cloth they'd used in the shelters into bags.

Now, the nearby mill put the flour into barrels instead of bags, and took the barrels to Philadelphia or the Delaware.

The mill—oh, how much it had been on everyone's mind once they heard that James Logan, ever the one with an eye on a promising investment, gave money to Christopher Schlegel to build a mill along a winding stream that flowed into the Conestoga Creek. Everyone now called it Mill Creek. Now, as long as they had wheat or rye, they could bake bread. In fact, most of them kept the rye for themselves because wheat sold for a higher price. He thought of Hans Groff from Germantown, who after looking several times, was purchasing 1,030 acres northeast of the Isaac LeFevre and Ferree tracts.

Christian whittled on the pegs in between soaking his sore leg. Father always kept a basket of square sticks or pegs of different sizes on hand. The one end was then rounded off so it could be put in a bored hole wherever one was needed when they were building. Martin Mylin was the blacksmith for all the settlers. He'd once learned the gunsmith skills and was now starting to repair guns and hoped to be making some soon.

The first apple trees would soon be bearing apples. Each homestead had planted some, but the biggest ones were, of course, the ones by the big spring.

Thinking of apples made him recall those peaches from the Indians four years ago. There hadn't been such a big crop since. In fact, two years ago there were only a few as a frost had gotten most of the blossoms. But the peaches in exchange for bread seemed to have broken the ice with the Indians and had left good feelings on both sides. All the families had planted peach stones and trees were growing now.

They had also learned another lesson three years ago. Queen Conquegas and some of her people had gone to Philadelphia with furs of bear, beaver, deer, fox, and raccoon. She reminded James Logan that Penn had promised that Christians and Indians would live as one body—one heart—one mind—one eye—and one ear.

Now the horses and hogs kept by Madame Ann Letort were getting into the corn of the Indians. But worse than that, some Indians had sat in her house for a visit and she had turned them out saying that it was her house and her land for she had bought it from William Penn. To the Indians, land belonged to everyone.

Christian remembered the advice from the ones at Skippack. Never lock your door to an Indian. Thus, all the settler's doors had remained unlocked and Indians were welcomed whenever they chose to enter. They had a strong feeling of sharing and if your neighbor had a snug cabin and a warm fire, they would share its warmth. If they killed a deer they might bring you a deer leg or a side if it was more then they needed.

But wise old Queen Conquegas had passed away now. Other Indians had reminded Logan that although the Indians did not write things down to keep records, they had their own ways to pass on the treaties and leagues and friendships that were made between the English and old Indian fathers.

Mother came in the door with several big leaves of Swiss Chard. She cut it up and added it to the rabbit stew. She looked at Christian's leg and nodded, "That looks better now. We don't want poisoning to set in, so take care of it."

"Ye-es — but the wheat!"

"Don't you worry yourself about the wheat. If that copperhead had bitten you, you probably would not be here to thank God that you are alive!"

Mother took a deep breath as she stirred the pot. "I've been thinking of the ones back home. Abraham's oldest, young Abraham, would be fifteen years old already and Rudolph would be fourteen. Then there is Christian, John, and Barbara." Mother wiped away a tear. "I get such a longing to see them again, and Emanuel and Isaac, too. I had hoped that by this time they would have come too. Of course, we will never know if they received any of the letters we sent or not since w receive no answers," she said.

"But we do know that Benedict Brechbühl moved to the village of Weiler at the foot of the Steinsberg and that he asked the Mennonites in Amsterdam in February 1714 for help because French soldiers had plundered the harvest again," said Christian, "and had also occupied parts of the Palatinate so that there was a shortage of food. So it must have probably been in the fall or winter of 1713 when the soldiers came. Having their harvest destroyed left them without the money to come even if they had planned to come. But maybe if they had a good harvest last year?"

"I just wish there was some way we could talk to them . . . but that's impossible," sighed Mother.

"What's impossible Mommy?" asked little Hans as he stood in the doorway. "Doddy said I can eat at your house today," he added.

Mother looked at her nine-year old grandson as she answered. "You ask what's impossible?" she sighed as Father and Anna and the children, John, and baby Christian, came in the door. "Why I was telling Christian here that I had hoped the rest of our children would have come over by now. If we could only talk to them and tell them what a blessed opportunity we have here—but that's not possible."

"But, yes, Mommy, that would be possible. Someone could just go over on a ship like the *Mary Hope* we came over on and tell them. Then they'd *have* to believe it."

Little Hans looked bewildered as everyone chuckled. "But why couldn't someone do that?

"We-ll-l, we'll have to think about it for a while," said Mommy as she went to the spring for a crock of milk and a crock of mulberries for dinner.

"Mommy, are we going to shake the mulberry trees again this evening?"

"Yes," said Mother, "I think we need to take the tow cloth out again and you can crawl up the tree and shake them for us."

Later that evening Christian said, "I've been thinking about what little Hans said. You know Martin Kendig has talked of his cousin Jacob who was interested in coming over and his two brothers. The last time I was in Germantown they said that Dielman Kolb, the youngest of the Kolb brothers wants to come over. They also said that Benedict Brechbühl was looking at land elsewhere in Europe to settle with his flock."

"They should all come here while the land is still available at good prices while Penn grants credit to our people."

"It is amazing how speculators have already bought up the land around us."

"Yes, true. Even that is a bargain yet."

"But, there are large areas of unclaimed lands north and northeast of here; and that land is just as good as this," said Christian.

"Yes," nodded Father. "At first I couldn't understand why such good land hadn't been taken earlier. But Isaac Taylor said they didn't want land that had such big trees to clear. Anyone who knows what good land is—knows it takes good land to grow big trees. Isaac Taylor says there was an Irishman by the name of Robert Gault who looked at this land, but went some miles south of here where the trees weren't so big and built a cabin there before we even came over. But to get back to little Hans' suggestion, why not bring it up with the rest at Sunday meeting? There's been a lot of talk ever since we found out about the French soldiers. Maybe the right time has come. But who would go?"

So the matter rested. But Christian talked with Martin Mylin the next day and little Hans told his parents how they had laughed at his remark. Hans told Wendell Bauman who thought it was a good idea and not to call impossible. Wendell Bauman asked Jacob Miller and Johann Anton Weber what they thought of the idea and by Sunday morning in one form or another, everyone knew about it already except for Martin Kendig.

"But, who should we send?" asked Christian. "Who will go? Of course, the rest of us will have to care for his family and crops while he is gone."

"Why not use the lot?" suggested Martin Kendig. "It's such a weighty matter, so shouldn't we let it in God's hands?"

There was a nodding of heads and Father said, "We need to make it a matter of prayer and give it more time. We don't want to be hasty. Are all of you agreed that it might be good to send a messenger over? Someone they know and trust? There have been so many golden glowing rumors that even William Penn was beguiled by Silver Mines that someone must have imagined."

"I also believe that the Indian massacre at New Bern, Carolina, has filtered back to the Palatinate and our friends too," said Hans.

One by one the men gave their "yea's."

Father asked, "What about the women?"

"We talked about it at home and Mother and Anna had no objections," said Christian.

The rest of the men nodded. Martin Kendig said, "I'll talk to my wife and we'll let you know. She has been wishing for more relatives and friends to come over, so I believe she'll agree as well."

So after the busy wheat harvest and then the rye harvest was over, all families assembled on a Sunday morning in *Herbstmonat* (September), and there was complete silence as Father and Johan Anton Weber lined up the songbooks on the table. One for every man there. One of them held the note, although no one knew whom as Father had turned his back as Johan Anton mixed up the books and Johan Anton turned his back as Father mixed up the books in the bedroom, then set them standing up on the table. Then there was prayer.

Anna let the tears flow knowing it could be Christian who would be chosen. Yet, the vision of those four ships that had gone to New York in 1709 kept rising before her eyes once again when 1,700 out of 4,000 had perished. And, the story of William Penn's first trip when smallpox had broken out and nearly one-third had died and Ann Letort, whose husband had been captured by the French warships, put into prison, and didn't come back for two years.

But, as Father prayed so calmly and earnestly that all be laid on the altar, a peace once more came into her heart. She thought of the fireflies and how they had taken care of her unnatural fears about bears and wolves. She still hated to hear the wolves howl in winter time, but at least she did not imagine them outside her door when they were miles away. Yes, God would see them through this mountain too — or, ocean was more like it, as Father prayed and said, "We know you rule the waves and the fog and the winds; so we ask you to rule our hearts and our tongues."

Then, it was the Lord's prayer, and Amen.

As one by one each took a book, one was left standing; Father's book. One by one he went and opened the books by age; the oldest one first.

The tension built up as he went around the benches. It was almost as if everyone was holding their breath as the last book was opened. But the note was not there. Calmly, Father lifted up the book still standing on the table. As he solemnly opened the book and picked up the note he had written and looked at the beloved faces around him, he was stunned.

Tears were flowing everywhere. Father swallowed a few times. He would usually call out a song to be sung for the closing of the service, but a weeping congregation could not sing. Softly, gently, he spoke the benediction and wordlessly they wandered to their homes.

Chapter Fourteen

It was a brisk March wind that howled around the log cabin as they ate breakfast by the light of the fire and a rush lamp. Mentally Christian went over the contents of the saddle bags once more to make sure he had everything they needed. It was full moon and they hoped to start off before dawn and travel in the light of the moon on the Conestoga Road near home. Anna sliced some cheese and wrapped it in a linen cloth and added it to the saddle bag.

"You know," said Christian, "when I think back to that day in September when the lot fell on Father . . ." he fell silent.

"Yes," sighed Anna, "I suppose it's one of those things we will never forget. What a feeling that was. Perhaps we'll pass that story on to our children and grandchildren, just as our ancestors passed on their stories of suffering for their faith. That numb feeling we had, to think of having Father chosen when they'd felt too old to come in the first place, and as our only minister . . . he was wanted and needed here."

Christian took a deep breath. "Yes, at least everyone agreed that we needed Father here, even though Father was willing to go. When Martin Kendig offered to take his place near Christmas time, everyone agreed then too. I was so thankful for that."

"But, do you know, it's hard to believe that in the nearly five years we've been here, Hans and I haven't visited Skippack once? We've met some of them a few times at Germantown and most have been here. But now, Martin Kendig wants to talk with the Kolb brothers because he's heard that Dielman Kolb, the youngest of the brothers, wants to come over."

"Be sure to remember how big their children are and remember what all to tell Gerhart Clemens and Ann and give a greeting to whoever asks about me. Someday, once the children are older, I hope to go along with you and spend several days visiting those families. I somehow felt a lot closer to those pioneering families than most of the ones at Germantown. Are you sure you have your five shillings for the quit rent?"

Christian nodded. "Yes, it's here in my pocket. Listen, I hear a horse. I believe that's Martin now." He lifted the saddle bags and headed for the horse tied in the barn ready to go.

"God go with you," said Anna as he was ready to mount. "Martin, our prayers will be with you," she said as they started off.

"Thanks Anna," he waved back.

As she watched them go to meet Hans she took a deep breath. "Oh God, guide them and protect them. It would be four or five days before they would return."

By starting out before dawn, they were hoping to reach Germantown by nightfall or at least travel as far as the Brandywine. They planned to visit Skippack on Saturday and spend Sunday there, and then travel to Philadelphia on Monday to pay their quit rent at James Logan's office. They would then go with Martin to the docks to see about a ship to sail to England. They would bring Martin's horse along home if all went as planned. So, it would be at least Tuesday before their families could expect them to return.

Their absence left a big hole on Sunday morning at meeting. Three men absent in such a small group was keenly felt. When the meeting was over, Martin Mylin said, "I think that as soon as they return, we should plan a meeting. We'll need to plan what we should do this year and next winter and so on. When do you expect them back?"

"Hopefully on Tuesday," said Father. "Why not get together at our place on Wednesday after dinner? That would allow a little extra time."

So they worked and waited and prayed. All afternoon Tuesday, Anna sat spinning where she could watch out the window. She made extra for supper in hopes Christian would be there. They waited awhile and finally ate without him.

Then, just as she finished the dishes, she heard something out at the barn. Quickly she grabbed her cloak and went out to meet him. "Here, hold Martin's horse for me, will you?" he asked Anna. "I'm afraid he'll try and run home," said Christian as he dismounted and untied Martin's horse from a rope on his saddle.

"What took so long?"

"Oh, everything! Down at the docks there were three ships leaving this week, so we bargained for the best price. You know, there are never many passengers to go back. One ship had lost some of their men who stayed here and if Martin was willing to help some, he could go for half-fare. You remember, we'd helped a bit on the way over when some of the crew were sick. And, Martin took extra food along," he said as they walked into the cabin together.

Once inside, Christian then repeated these things to Father and Mother.

"Then we had dinner at Jan Lensen's on Monday. We could hardly get away. He told each of us to prepare to feed at least three extra families the next winter. He said, 'Next year, after the wheat harvest is in, plant a lot of extra turnips. If you don't need them, feed them to the cattle.' The Kolb brothers told us the same, 'Be prepared for quite a lot more families.' They said 'Now is the time you need to pass on the help we gave you. The land that you've cleared over winter that's not planted in wheat, plant that in cabbage, Indian corn, squash, pumpkins, and buckwheat.'"

"Yes, but where will we find seed for so much?" asked Mother.

Christian chuckled. "They'll give us a lot of extra seed. The Kolbs and their neighbors will give some turnip seeds, and Jan Lensen will give extra flax seed, and his wife will give a lot of extra onion, cabbage, and beet seeds. Jan said he and the other weavers will buy back the spun flax the next spring so they can earn extra, just as we did six years ago."

Anna nodded. "They'll want heifers too, I suppose, and cows and oxen and horses?"

"Yes," nodded Father, "we should let the Brethren down there know for next year to save any cows or heifers or horses until after they come over. We have some extra now, but not enough if a lot of families arrive. But, it's bedtime. We'll need to go over all this again tomorrow anyhow, when the rest gather here after dinner."

Christian raised his eyebrows and nodded, "Good!"

Anna would have wanted to talk yet, but soon saw he was too tired. Her questions would have to wait.

The next afternoon they all gathered together. Elizabeth Kendig, her daughter, and her son John Jacob came too. They would take Martin's horse along home. They were eager to hear how Martin's plans had turned out. "The Kolb brothers wrote a letter for their brother saying they'll line up a place for him and will get ready to build."

Then Christian told of the advice from the Kolb brothers and Jan Lensen, to plant a lot extra crops next year. "We may have to use most of our wheat for food and all of the rye," said John Funk, "if Martin brings his two brothers over that he's mentioned, as well as a cousin or two."

"We are hoping that Abraham and his family, and Emanuel and Isaac will come too. That's one family and two singles right there. If Benedict Brechbühl and his flock should all decide to come, and I hope they do, then we'll have an elder or bishop here. But, that could be at least one or two dozen families or even a lot more."

Mother spoke up, "I'll try and raise the onion sets this year to plant next year. That takes a lot of weeding and if they send the seed, I'll try and do that. We'll make raised beds to plant them, and that will make it easier to weed."

Then, one by one, they offered to plant more. Most had cleared about one to two acres over winter and they could do that next winter too. They could then plant beans, extra cabbage, Indian corn, and buckwheat as Jan Lensen had suggested.

"I'll try to raise a lot of extra cabbage plants," suggested Anna, "that we can plant after wheat if we need to. At least, some of the late cabbage."

Father said, "I'll try to make extra rye straw baskets and extra pegs for building. We men can all work on shingles over the winter once there's time after they come over, if we live and the Lord wills."

"I can make extra nails in my shop," said Martin Mylin, "and I'll try to make some guns."

John Funk spoke up, "Have you considered that we'll need more cellar space to store all this food?"

Several men raised their heads and nodded.

"Yes," said Father, "Christian, you have talked of building a stone house sometime where you have an arch cellar. Could you build a larger arch cellar where you plan to build the house?"

"But . . . but . . . we won't have the time to build a house, with all we have to do to prepare for them, and then we'll be building for those who come the next year."

"Yes," said Father, "but if we build a much larger arch cellar this spring yet, you could just put the earth back over it, instead of a house."

Several men nodded. "We could start this week yet. The frost is out of the ground. Why don't we walk up there now and see how we should make it?" suggested George Miller.

It was finally decided to build a larger part at the back end on the west. They'd take out most of the back wall and reuse the stones. The top at the back end would be above ground level later once the house was built and would contain some ventilation slits for use once the vent in the front was closed off with the house. It was planned to gather the next day to dig it out.

A week later it had been dug out. They had removed quite a lot of rocks that would be used in the walls. In fact, there was one place on the south side where there was bedrock they couldn't even remove. The men advised Christian to build his fireplace on the large rock towards the south, once the house was built.

Christian nodded, "That's about the right place for the central fireplace anyway."

Then work halted as the ground became fit to plant oats and flax. The plowing was done for the Indian corn and the gardens were planted. They all planted more peas and beans so they'd have extra for seed next year, and more root crops to grow seeds for the new settlers. Extra efforts were put forth to clear more ground for fall wheat and rye planting, so there would be enough.

Powder, shot, and salt were things they couldn't do vey well without. The other household things and the tools that had been most needed, they had purchased in the past five years.

By fall, when there was stock taken of the harvest, there was good news on the beans and Indian corn, and most of the rye and wheat harvest. It had been rather dry in May and June. The straw was shorter, yet had yielded a fair crop of grain. Only the peas were in short supply, so it was decided to put most of those away for seed. There was a bountiful crop of the later beans when rains had come. Enough to eat and a lot extra to plant. They had also planted extra buckwheat seed and had a fair crop of that. They worked at making beds for the onion seeds and cabbage plants, adding leaf mold and rotted manure in the fall.

Some of the women helped to flail out wheat and rye that winter instead of spinning, in order to give the men more time to clear land. A few people built an extra summerhouse that could be used as temporary living quarters if needed. Father's loom was busy all winter, with Christian at times taking over making tow cloth for bed ticks when the weather wasn't fit to clear land.

By springtime, there was a lot of speculation about which of their relatives and friends might come. Whenever they got together, they spoke of relatives, especially the women. A longing to see and talk with them, knowing that now was about the time they would be leaving.

Elizabeth Kendig said, "I can just imagine the scenes. What shall we take and what must we leave behind that we really don't want to? Not just in one household, but in every one," she said forcefully.

"Well, Martin can be a rather convincing speaker," added Father. "Just suppose so many come it will seem like Moses and the Israelites . . ."

There were smiles all around. "Well, they have an Atlantic Ocean to cross instead of a desert, but unless God's blessings are given, our plans will be in vain," said Christian.

Frances sighed, "I think all these plans of raising extra food have been on my mind too much because one night I dreamt we had such good weather and the very biggest and best crops we had ever seen," she took a deep breath, "and then nobody came! Martin came home alone and said, 'They'll come next year.' Then I woke up."

There was a lot of chuckling and Frances laughed sheepishly. "Oh, but you should just have seen those big cabbages," she said, making a circle as large as her arms could reach. Again there were amused smiles.

"Were they as large as the grape bunches Joshua and Caleb and the ten spies brought home?"

"Well, I've never seen such big cabbages, that's for sure," smiled Frances, "and I don't expect I ever will."

That summer the weather and rains were much more on everybody's mind than usual. There was a lot of extra weeding to do. Anna planted her beds of cabbage seeds and was greatly pleased when John Miller brought along a copper sprinkling can that Christian had ordered for her. She made several different plantings and spread powdered lime and wood ashes on them to away the bugs and worms away.

On his next trip, John Miller also brought more news of the Palatinate. The old Prince had died and the new elector, a Catholic, called the Mennonites 'a plague' in his realm. He had raised their special taxes, was trying to reduce the number of their households, and refused permission for the young men to enter trades.

They said they dug up their old tax receipts and legal papers that they had buried when the French came through, but could no longer read them.

Everyone took a deep breath. Christian said, "Here I'd been thinking quite often that perhaps we have planted too much . . . but with that news . . . I'm quite sure we didn't plant enough."

"What all can we still plant," asked Anna, "besides turnips?"

Mother took a deep breath. "Well, a lot of lettuce and beans and beets, there's seed here for those yet. We need to plant turnips every few days in case some don't come up well. We've been blessed with good rains just now and things should come up well. We could use your new watering can to sprinkle the beets," said Mother, "and I thought you had far too many cabbage plants left over. If we can, we should plant them all with this news we received."

"I think you should take the horse and let all the rest know of our plans," said Father. "They can come for more cabbage plants whenever they are ready, or more lettuce, bean, beet, and turnip seeds."

As August came, there was much talk of when they might come. "Well, it was September 23 when we came to Philadelphia. It might be September 1st or evenOctober sometime," said Father. "We'll just have to work and trust and pray and let it rest in God's hands."

"Well you know, we were at London for ten weeks! If they don't have to wait that long there, it might be a lot sooner."

On August 12, Mother and Anna were out in the garden weeding the new beets when two riders rode in. As they went out to meet them, they were both puzzled. "There is something familiar about both of them," said Anna, as the riders dismounted. Then suddenly, she stopped in her tracks and her mouth fell open and her arms went limp at her side. It was brother Emanuel! She looked at Mother behind her who was still unaware of who it was.

"Don't you know me?" asked the other boy. "I'm Henry Rittenhouse." Anna nodded. Emanuel stepped forward and thought his Mother was about to faint and grabbed her. "Mother, Mother, weren't you expecting me?" he asked.

Once Mother got her breath she said, "Why yes, we were hoping . . . hoping for so long . . . that now it is hard to believe. Where is Abraham and his family? And Issac?"

"Abraham and his family are probably all at Germantown resting. Barbara wanted very badly to come with me, but Anna was afraid she wasn't strong enough yet. But where is Father? And Christian, and Hans? And is this little Hans?" he asked in surprise.

"Soon, you can't call him little Hans anymore."

"Hans," said Anna, "go tell the men to come."

Before long Hans came running back. "John Miller was there too on his horse and he left to notify everyone else."

Once Father, Hans, and Christian had greeted Emanuel and Henry, Mother said, "You told me about Abraham and all but you didn't mention Isaac."

Emanuel sighed, "Isaac offered to be the one to come later. We couldn't scrape together the funds for all of us. But he felt if he farmed the land we left, he should be able to earn enough in one or two years, so we left what we could for him to farm." Mother bowed her head and a few tears came.

"Did Benedict Brechbühl and his flock come?" asked Father.

"Yes, and also elder (bishop) Hans Burkholder and elder Valentine Klemmer. But Klemmer has relatives in Bucks County and plans to settle there. But Martin Kendig sent us up here to tell you to send all the wagons down and any extra horses. Henry here, will ride on behind. Send some food too and some bed ticks for the children to sleep and ride on."

Just then John Jacob Kendig rode up and wanted news about his Father. When he heard that all was well, he rode back to tell his Mother and sister who were walking.

"Why not give Emanuel and Henry a bite to eat until everyone is here," said Father, as people started asking questions.

In an unbelievably short time, the whole community was there. Once they had all gathered, Father asked, "Were all the people on one ship?"

"No, there were three shiploads of us."

"Three — three — THREE!" echoed through the group.

"Did my brother come?" asked John Funk.

"Martin Kendig gave me a list of names. There's a Jacob and Henry Funk on the list."

"Any Baumans?" asked Wendell.

"There's a John and Michael. There's a George, Henry, and Jacob Kendig, and Jacob, Jr."

"How many were on the three ships?" asked Christian.

"Three hundred and sixty-three people!"

Again, a wave of surprise and ohs and ahs went through the group. Three hundred and sixty-three people to feed and help!

"But not all expect to settle here. Maybe sixty or sixty-five families. At least that many, but it might be more. The ones with relatives at Skippack or Swamp in Bucks County expect to go there."

Hans looked at Frances. All summer they had referred to her dream time and again. He chuckled at the big smile on her face and said softly, "I think we need big cabbages."

Frances only nodded and smiled some more.

Emanuel cleared his throat. "There'll be several wagons coming up from Germantown Martin said, but not until next week. He said if you have wheat or flour to send along back, send it."

"The wheat and flour will probably all be needed here," said Father. "Let us bow our heads and have a prayer of thanks to our great and merciful God for a safe trip here."

CHAPTER FIFTEEN

It was Sunday afternoon and Anna and the children had gone for a walk. Mother and Father were at Abraham's for a few weeks. Christian thought back to August 1717, as he often did. It was a time none of them would ever forget. The new arrivals came from Germantown, thirty, forty, or even fifty at a time; fortunately, not everyone came at once. Even so, wave after wave of people came. There was only one bake oven in the community, and it was being used six days a week for quite awhile. Fortunately, everyone had a big cooking pot by this time, and they all were certainly needed.

How thankful everyone was that they had had rain in September and October. On every farm the turnips had grown large, and farmers had dug pits in which to store them. Some of the turnips were covered with cloth, with straw on top of it, then covered with a layer of earth so the farmers could retrieve them when the ground was frozen. The arch cellars weren't nearly big enough, so farmers also took wagonloads of turnips to the new homesteads where people had buried them. Once the weather was cold, all the men banded together and went further north and east and had a drive to hunt bear and deer. That had been a big help.

Because they had come so early and there was a lot of help, most of the larger families built cabins yet that fall. Most had also planted rye. Some immigrants had brought tents, but they were already looking to buy land when Governor Keith's agents caught up with them. The new governor was a bit alarmed that three shiploads of German immigrants had come without completing any forms or registrations, or signed any Oath of Loyalty to the British King or its equivalent.

The agent told the immigrants that they had to appear before a magistrate within a month and affirm their loyalty to the British King. On September 25, Christian had gone with Hans Funk to Germantown. The next day they applied for 5,000 acres of land for several families. They agreed to pay the down payment for the land.

Isaac Taylor received instructions to lay out 5,000 more acres of land, even though he was already busy laying out a manor of 16,500 acres for the Penn family to keep it off the market. In reality, the land was a place for the Indians to live and hunt in peace; the Indians were very well pleased.

Isaac Taylor also had been annoyed with the new German immigrants because they had not given much heed to regulations. He told them, "You must come under normal regulations or you will get no land at all." At least Taylor knew that the Mennonites would pay for their land and not "squat" on it without paying as the Scotch Irish had done in the past.

When Isaac Taylor thought he was finished in the fall, Hans Groff's horses had run away and Hans had tracked them several miles further northeast. There Hans had found a very strong spring. He had seen such big trees there that he decided he wanted 1,000 or more acres in that area.

The Mennonites had settled rather heavily around the Mill Creek area where speculators had bought land in 1711 and 1712. James

Logan had once again financed a mill for Quaker Edmund Cartledge along Mill Creek. Brother Emanuel had bought 500 acres of Tract No. 1 that Martin Kendig had in his name. Elder Benedict Brechbühl and Christian Shenk had split up Tract No. 2, which John Funk had purchased before he obtined some of Wendell Bauman's land, and built a cabin there. Brechbühl and Shenk built their cabins near each other.

Most of the first settlers' cabins had been rather crowded that winter during the coldest weather. Those who had no cabins had rough shelters which were satisfactory in mild weather, but once it got really cold they were glad there were cabins that were warmer and built more tightly.

There were several hogs to butcher that winter, and they sure were needed. The cows had no squash, pumpkins, or turnips to eat that winter. Farmers had to make a few more drives for deer; they also spent more time fishing. None of the families went hungry, even if all they had were turnips, cabbage or sauerkraut, Indian porridge, and some meat day after day, sometimes with a few buckwheat cakes and bread.

The first settlers were reminded of their own first winter. They had had to sell quite a bit of wheat in order to purchase salt to cure their meat that year. Many of their peas and beans were saved to plant the next year, and some of the rye had been needed for planting, too.

James Logan had sent large wagonloads of nails, hinges, glass windows, and tools to the Letort Trading Post since some settlers had money to purchase them. He thought of the herd of heifers and cows that were driven from Skippack, Germantown, and Swamp. Logan's old friend Gerhart Clemens' son, Jacob, helped deliver the herd. A few of the new settlers had said that they needed a cow, but had no money to pay for one.

Young Jacob Clemens had told them, "When our father came here about ten years ago in October, he bought a horse from Hendrick Kassel for three pounds, seven shillings, and six pence, but he did not have to pay until the following May." He said his father still has the paper. Over the winter his mother did spinning and his father obtained enough furs to pay for the horse. So for those who had no money, a note was made as to whose heifer it was and how much the settler would have to pay once he had enough money.

Christian got the paper with the list of new settlers out of his Bible. Some of the names were: Melchior and Christopher Brenneman; Jacob Brubaker; two Hans Brubakers; Theodorus Eby; Melchior

Erisman; Elder Hans Burkholder; Hans Brand; George, Henry, and two Jacob Kendigs, who were two of Martin Kendig's brothers and a cousin.

Christian smiled as he recalled how Benedict Brechbühl had said that Martin Kendig was so convincing while he was in the Palatinate. *"Ich hap ein house fon lauter niss bleck.* (I have a house of all walnut logs.)" Others on the list were John and Benjamin Witmer; John Witwer; Michael Bachman; Hans, Henry, and Martin Bare; Hans Conrad; Hans Rudolph; Jacob Moyer; Michael Miller; Henry and Jacob Funk; John Forrer; Peter Beller; Michael Denlinger; Peter Swarr; Hans Newcomer; Hans Henrich Neff, the old doctor; Andrew and Michael Kauffman (Michael had passed away); Jacob Hoober; Jacob Hochstetter; two Hans Nissleys; Jacob Martin; Christian, John, and two Michael Shenks; Christian Schantz; Hans Newcomer; Hans and Martin Byer; Isaac Frederic; John Forrer; Joseph Stehman; Hans Snider; Christian Steiner; Felix and two Jacob Landis'; Peter Lehman; Henry Mussleman; Hans and Jacob Mylin; Christian, Benjamin, and Ulrich Hershey; Hans Keagy; Hans Hess; Hans and Ulrich Hauri; and Jacob Krieder. "I'm not sure I got them all, but most of them. I forgot to add Benedict Brechbühl to my list."

Christian sighed. "No wonder we felt almost overwhelmed." There were over seventy families once they all arrived last fall; some said about seventy-six.

No wonder Brother Hans, Martin Kendig, and John Funk had to go to Philadelphia to ask for 6,000 more acres. This was granted by the commissioner on November 22, 1717, because they considered the people whom Martin had brought over to be "honest, conscientious people." The commissioners agreed to lay out these acres wherever the people chose land. They were granted a rare privilege not everyone received.

Peter Bezaillion's road was used by many to find springs or creeks farther northwest of "Neu Strasburg," as it was now being called, and all along the Conestoga. Plans were now being made to build the new stone house. They had started to quarry stones about 200 steps northeast of the house where they had dug down and found them. With so many settlers coming over, there was a lot of help available, including a stonemason.

Father had suggested that they make the stone house large enough so they could hold meetings there. So they made it 30x38 feet. The house would have a large central fireplace, perhaps ten feet long, so Anna could have a German-raised hearth and use a small fire for each cooking pot. There would be a small bedroom off the kitchen for the children, or used as a storage room for tools and food. There would also be a larger bedroom and the *stube* which had a heating stove that was fired from the fireplace in front through an opening in the stone wall of the fireplace. Logs were started in the fireplace, then the red embers placed in the plastered stone stove. Anna dreamed of a smoke-free, warm room in which to live, eat, and work, and then on Sundays gather together for meetings and worship.

Christian nodded to himself as he visualized how he planned to make the stove. It would be surrounded by a bench where you could sit when you came in from the cold. It was a place where you could hang your coat after being out in the rain, hang laundry to dry, place food to warm on a ledge, or bake a custard or pudding in a pottery dish. Christian thought about the family eating their meals together at the table in the *stube*. He could imagine Anna at her spinning wheel while Father sat whittling or making straw baskets.

Mother wasn't spinning anymore; she was braiding the rye straw for straw hats. She kept the cut rye straw, which had the joints cut out, in a damp linen cloth, and she braided long braids and loops of the straw for straw hats for the neighborhood in summertime. Men's hats were made with a large crown, and women's hats were made nearly flat and tied under the chin. These were worn for gardening and helped keep them cool especially during the wheat harvest.

Mother and Father were slowing down, especially in the last year or so. Somehow it seemed they had pushed themselves too hard in the summer and fall of 1717. *We all did*, mused Christian to himself. *But we younger people could recover more quickly. But how would it have gone if we hadn't*, thought Christian. *Would everyone have gone hungry at times? Because we couldn't have had plenty for ourselves and let others starve.*

He thought of the many onions that Mother, Frances, and the rest had planted. Those were just ready to dig when the settlers had first come, and Mother had put the women to work braiding onions into strings. Even so, they had eaten all the onions before spring came and game did not taste as good when it was cooked without onions. At least Mother's onion seedlings had done well and the new settlers had plenty of onion sets for planting. Father had planned to have enough rye straw baskets to give each new settler a basket filled with onion sets. He didn't have enough but the settlers had helped him, too. They had plenty of straw and each had received one or more baskets.

How everyone had rejoiced when the Brethren from Germantown and Skippack had sent all those bags of dried apples. What a treat that had been. Christian well remembered how he and Benedict Brechbühl had spent several days delivering the bags of apples to all the new settlers' places. No one had received a lot of them, but all were so happy to receive what they did. Christian often wondered if the thoughtfulness and caring of the Brethren, most of whom the settlers had never met, hadn't meant as much or more than the food. The love of the Brethren—how it bound them together. He was so glad he had asked Benedict to help deliver the apples. Benedict had a gift for showing God's love in the way he spoke to people.

Christian had planned to be finished delivering the dried apples much sooner, but he soon saw that the settlers were just as hungry for spiritual food and encouragement as they were for the apples. These families were going through a lot of adjustments, yet they also knew what Benedict had suffered for his faith.

It seemed rather foolish to complain of having only turnips three times a day to eat with a bit of meat and Indian corn. When Benedict had been in prison, he worked where it was cold, and had only bread and water to eat. It made no sense to complain of howling wolves, when Benedict had been in leg chains and was sent nearly 3,000 miles away from his family. *Benedict's words carried more weight than anything I could have said or done,* he thought to himself, *even if I had used the same words he did.*

Yes, Benedict had suffered much, but his faith, his obvious caring, and overflowing love had been multiplied because if it. He had breathed new spiritual life into the community and new life into the singing, too. His clear, bell-like voice had been a gift from God. Benedict's use of it in service and praise to God was service to God and his fellow man. Christian knew it was a special privilege to have such a man for a good friend and neighbor.

Christian thought of Benedict's special Bible which he had been given because some pages had been damaged, and how he had patched and restored it with beautiful hand lettering. The Bible was one of the very first Froschauer editions that had been printed in 1531. Benedict had also translated part of a Dutch book titled *Die Wandlende Seele* (*The Wandering Soul*).

Christian looked out the window and saw Anna and the children coming.

"What have you been doing?" she asked.

"Oh, I've been thinking back over last year and all the people who came, and how hard we worked to grow a lot of food. We thought we had much more than we needed, but it was hardly enough. If it hadn't been for the meat we got on those hunting drives and the fish, we would have run short by the time spring foods were available. Even so, some had mostly fish and wild greens for awhile until the garden crops came in."

"Yes," nodded Anna, "I still have to smile every time I think of how those boys pulled such a joke on Frances with her big cabbage."

Christian nodded and chuckled. "I asked some of the boys later what gave them the idea, and they said it was our talk of the ten spies and how big the grapes were. So they decided to see if they could help Frances grow as big a cabbage as she had dreamed about."

"I didn't know that was what gave them the idea, but they didn't tell John Miller about it until they found out that one had added well-rotted manure to the cabbage row, and another added fish heads and trimmings. Then the boys were afraid it would be too much fertilizer. John helped them give the cabbage a lot more room by moving the plant. That's what made a big difference, too—it had lots of room to grow so big."

"Plus the fact that the boys watered the plant with that cracked crock every time they went by."

Little John piped up, "Yes, and twice Aunt Frances almost caught them at it. Then when you caught them giving the plant water, they had to tell you what they were trying to do."

"What amused me," said Christian, "was that Hans had noticed that one cabbage was so much bigger than the rest. Whenever he mentioned anything to Frances, she felt she was being teased about her dream and just said she was too busy to go look."

"Yes, then one Sunday when we were all there, the boys went out to the garden and came back and told Frances that at least a part of her dream had come true. There was a cabbage out there that was as big as she could reach around," laughed John.

"When Frances saw it, she said right away, 'Something is fishy here!' The boys' laughter gave them away. They had planned to pretend that the big cabbage had grown by itself, but Frances saw that the plant wasn't even at the end of the row where she had planted it. They had moved it. Then she checked under the leaves and saw they had made a little dam to hold all the water they gave it. Then Frances got the whole story and everyone talked about 'this promised land' where, if you work extra hard, you can grow cabbages so big you can hardly carry them."

"That reminds me, Anna," said Christian, "I promised Abraham's children I would tell them some of Martin Chartier's stories that he told us at the blacksmith shop. You know he went along to explore a river called the Mississippi that is hundreds of miles west of here? It flows all the way from Canada, thousands of miles to a place called the Gulf of Mexico."

"I had hoped that sometime the children could hear the stories from Martin, but now that he passed away in May, they won't get the chance."

"Yes," sighed Anna, "and William Penn has gone to his reward, too. Some have said his sons are to share Pennsylvania and that they don't have Penn's deep faith or sense of justice and fairness, so I wonder . . . "

"Yes," sighed Christian, "at least William Penn was a man who made the world a better place for many, even though it brought him a lot of trouble. Others reap where he planted. I wish he would have outlawed slavery, but at least he started a worship meeting for the slaves. Shahaise told me that the Indians still have the parchment treaty Penn gave them. He had told the Indians to preserve it for three generations."

Anna took a deep breath. "I'm so glad I never knew that in the bitter war with the local Indians, and the Five Nations way back in about 1650, that each side burned alive the captives of the other side."

"Yes," nodded Christian, "most European people would call the Indians uncivilized or barbarians, not seeming to realize that Anabaptists suffered the same fate because they refused to give up their faith. That reminds me, Anna. Why don't we eat an early supper and walk over to Benedict Brechbühl's this evening? He mentioned some church history that I'm not sure I've heard."

Later that evening, Brother Emanuel joined them on their walk to Benedict's house.

"With the dry weather we've had this fall," said Christian, "we can easily cross the Pequea Creek. Last fall it was running strong and full at this time."

Emanuel nodded. "We sure were blessed by those rains last fall. We might have gone a bit hungry if it hadn't rained and given us such a good turnip harvest. It's certainly a relief now that all the cabins have been built, and most of the wheat is planted, too. We could use some rain—that light sprinkle we had last week sure helped."

Benedict and his family were glad to see the visitors when they arrived. When Christian asked about some church history, Benedict smiled and said, "How much do you know?"

"Well, I know that Conrad Grebel, Felix Manz, and George Blaurock were the first leaders, but you mentioned in one of your sermons names from earlier centuries."

Benedict nodded. "Unfortunately, the *Martyr's Mirror* has never been translated from the Dutch. It contains stories from martyrs from every century, I believe."

"You spoke about Peter Waldo and the Waldensians."

Benedict cleared his throat and stroked his beard. "I don't believe Peter Waldo founded the group, but he was probably its most important leader. About five hundred or more years ago, he paid a priest to translate the Gospels and a number of other New Testament books into French. Waldo was a merchant who gave away his goods to the poor and chose instead to preach the scriptures to all willing to listen. They were also known as 'the poor men of Lyons.' From there they spread over Europe, and endured the same persecution our people did, or even worse. The group believed in simplicity and holiness, and most of what we believe. There were still remnants of these people in Bohemia, Germany, Moravia, and Switzerland when the Reformers arose, such as Martin Luther and Ulrich Zwingli, and later John Calvin.

"Many of these people followed the Reformers at first. Later, when they realized they were compromising to favor the civil authorities because the civil authorities did not want to lose control of the church, many were not satisfied and joined the Anabaptists, who desired separation of church and state. They were a group of believers who favored adult baptism on faith and nonresistance as taught in the scriptures."

Christian nodded. "Then, you also mentioned about some Brethren from Thessalonica."

"If I understand correctly, about 1540 there were Swiss Brethren living in Moravia. They were visited by three Brethren from Thessalonica, and discovered that their faith and the way it was practiced was so much alike that they shared a communion service together. It appears that the Thessalonica group had been there for a long time; some feel perhaps even from the time of the Apostles. We don't know for sure.

"But going back to the early Reformers, most of the ones who made the most impact were Peter Waldo, who had translations of the scriptures done in the language of the people; and John Wycliffe who had a great impact about 400 years ago by producing the first translation of the Bible into the English language. Wycliffe's followers were called Lollards. They took their Bibles and preached to England's poor people.

"Later, John Huss was a follower of Wycliffe and preached so much against the corruption of the church that he was burned at the stake."

Emanuel nodded. "And Martin Luther translated the Bible into the German language."

"Yes," sighed Benedict, "our people have always preferred the older Froschauer edition, but here they are almost impossible to find. Unless things change, if one wants a German Bible we may have to accept Martin Luther's translation now."

Christian saw Anna's worried glance at the setting sun. He rose and said as they started to leave, "I think we'd better start for home if we want to be able to see the path. We hope to work on the fireplace tomorrow."

"I hear the Indians are interested in all the stone you are quarrying," said Benedict.

"Yes," nodded Christian. "The Indian men and the boys as well. I've a notion to get the boys to help load and unload the stones when we transport them with the stone sled. Maybe if Anna has some good bread and adds some of that apple butter we made last week, they'll help us!"

*   *   *

During the next summer Christian often thought of those words as he worked at plastering the fireplace. By now he had learned enough of the Indian language that he could converse fairly well with the Indian boys. Of course, sign language was resorted to at times as well.

The boys had wanted to know why he built such a big fireplace. Christian had tried to explain. Why did he build a stone house? He had told the boys it was warmer in winter and would last much longer. They had loved Anna's bread and apple butter, and gladly helped him and Emanuel pick up fieldstones and bring some from the quarry, in exchange for some of the treat.

As Christian plastered over the stones on the fireplace, he took the square end of a peg and traced in his initials—C. H. The "H" was crooked, and he smeared over it with his hand and tried again, then nodded in approval. He stood back and surveyed his home. The high roof line provided for both a second floor and an attic in the peak. Heavy beams were added to brace the attic floor so that wheat could be stored there, away from the rats and mice. Father had made the wooden attic stairs. Each step was a whole hewn log and pegged on a squared-off log. Father remembered the same kind of log staircase that they had had back in Switzerland. The staircase was now finished and ready to install.

He thought about the door lintel he had carved last winter from a long piece of sandstone: ƻ 7CH HR 19. The backward ƻ meant AD 1719. Someone had asked about the lintel and how they worked to get the letters right. Tomorrow they would have a group to work on the floors. They had worked on the floorboards most of last winter using a drawing knife. On Sunday a special church service was planned where Benedict would take counsel about ordaining another minister. He sighed as he thought to himself, *There's no one here who can measure up to Benedict Brechbühl in so many ways. But whoever it will be, will at least have the privilege of learning from Benedict and working under him.*

Christian took a deep breath as he thought of the benches different men had been making to use for meetings. The house still needed a lot of work until all the plastering was done. The boards had been split last winter. They would be wrapped in rye straw that was dipped in a mud mixture of red clay and cattle dung, and placed between the joists. The boards would then be plastered over with a mixture of sand, lime, and wood ashes to which cattle hair had been mixed. This would help keep the house warmer. Then it would be whitewashed.

So many people had helped build the house, including the Indian boys who had helped haul stones. Christian sensed that had given the boys a feeling of being welcome in the house. That was the way he wanted it. One boy had even asked that if it got really cold and the snow was deep, could they sleep by the fire, when he had made a small fire in the fireplace.

Christian told the boys, "All the children of God or the Great Spirit are welcome here." They nodded their understanding. As Christian thought of the Indians, his thoughts went to what Immigrant Jacob Kreider had told him. In 1717, Jacob had brought a tent when he was first living near the Conestoga. He then made a rough shelter from hickory saplings covered with bark; the shelter also had a fireplace. Indians had come to Jacob to visit and trade fish and game for bread. On one such visit, Jacob was looking at his almanac and saw that there soon would be an eclipse of the moon. He told this to the Indians and when it was to occur. On that night fifty or sixty Indians came and saw it happen.

They were awed, and after a breathtaking view in silence, one said, "Tis the white man's God that tells him this, or else he would not know it."

Then the next evening, John Miller came home from Philadelphia with his wagon, bringing their brother Isaac. How they all rejoiced!

Mother said, "My cup runneth over."

Soon Hans and Christian went to Philadelphia to apply for land for Isaac. Even though they were well known at the land office by now, the officials were reluctant to grant any more lands just now because of William Penn's death and the uncertainties there were about who was in charge. It wasn't until October 1719 that Hans and Abraham went again to Philadelphia, and 400 acres were then surveyed for Isaac.

A little over two weeks later the new stone house was full of people, more than the number that usually gathered for Sunday meeting services. Elder Hans Burkholder was there, too. They talked about so many things: Christ and the Cross; the faith and persecution of their ancestors; God's providence in so many ways and in so many things.

Christian's thoughts traveled far and wide along with the minister's as they discussed the Old Testament and on to the New Testament. They talked about the qualifications of a minister and his wife, and the use of the lot. Then they had prayer, and almost before he realized what was happening, Benedict Brechbühl reached for the book in Christian's hand.

It seemed to Christian as if his heart stopped beating when he opened the book and read the note: *Berufen zum diener des worts* (called to preach the Word). It was overwhelming, as first Benedict gave Christian a Holy kiss and Godly admonition, then Hans Burkholder and the rest.

Hans and Frances had been the last to leave. Hans had reminded Christian of the words that Father had written in his New Testament.

What should one chiefly seek in this book? To recognize Jesus Christ, the man of righteousness, and believe in Him; for Christ is the true, noble treasure concealed in the field of the Holy Scripture. Him should one seek. Whoever finds Him and holds to Him with true faith, he will not be lost but shall have eternal life. John 3:16.

Conclusion

In growing up, I had many questions about our area of Lancaster County, and how and why and by whom it was settled. What about the Indians who first lived here? It became more exciting when I discovered that our farm bordered Peter Bezaillion's trail, and that Peter's Road was named for Peter Bezaillion.

My search for answers brought us in contact with Amos B. Hoover at the Muddy Creek Farm Library who suggested that I write a book. He shared lots of information to get me started. I wrote three chapters, but there it rested for over fifteen years.

When Raymond and Darvin Martin's work on the history and genealogy of the Martins was published; and they expressed their concern for books for children and teenagers, it renewed my interest in this project.

Then when John Ruth's 1,300-page book, *The Earth is the Lords*, was printed in 2001, I finally had the resources at my fingertips to write such a book. The Mennonite history as well as the Amish division details comes from this book. Indian history and information on William Penn came from Dunaway's *History of Pennsylvania*.

Steve Friesen's *A Modest Mennonite Home* and Samuel Wenger's *The Wenger Book* that showed the land tracts of the first 10,000-acre settlement, plus the tour that Wenger gave us, were all invaluable. Thank you to all of these people for permission to use this information. The Lancaster Mennonite Historical Society also provided valuable reference sources to document this story, although there are certain facts like the ordination date for Christian Herr that we could not locate.

I. Daniel Rupp wrote the first history of Lancaster County in 1844. Rupp spoke and read about five languages and conscientiously gathered information from more than one source to document his data. He began compiling information in 1827 by talking with the old people from the Pequea to the Conestoga.

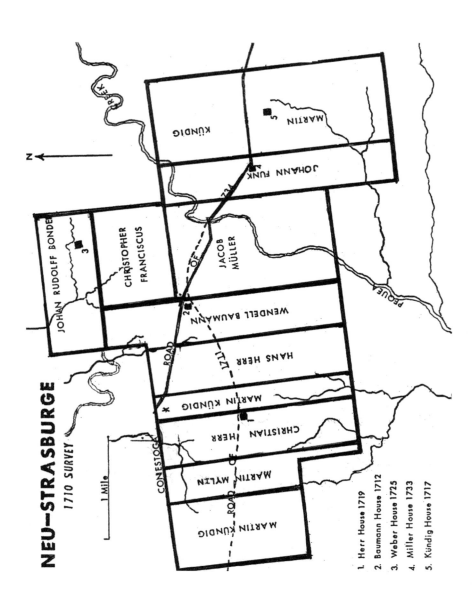

NEU–STRASBURGE
1710 SURVEY

N ←

1 Mile

CONESTOGA

MARTIN KÜNDIG

MARTIN MYLIN

ROAD OF

CHRISTIAN HERR

MARTIN KÜNDIG

HANS HERR

WENDELL BAUMANN

JACOB MÜLLER

CHRISTOPHER FRANCISCUS

JOHAN RUDOLFF BONDE

ROAD

OF

JOHANN FUNK

KÜNDIG

MARTIN

CREEK

PEQUEA

1. Herr House 1719
2. Baumann House 1712
3. Weber House 1725
4. Miller House 1733
5. Kündig House 1717

Christian and Anna Herr built the Hans Herr House in 1719. Their granddaughter, Barbara Herr, inherited the homestead when she was eighteeen years old and soon thereafter married Henry Shaub in 1772. Barbara (Herr) Shaub owned this homestead for over fifty years until 1823 when she sold it to her son, Christian Shaub. Barbara was fourteen years old when her Grandma Anna Herr died in 1768 and certainly was influenced by many memories of working and learning to know her Immigrant Grandma—memories which she held for the ninety-five years of her life until she died in 1846. She lived all of her life, or else a few hundred feet away, in the Hans Herr House. It seems very probable that Rupp visited and talked with Barbara who would have shared a wealth of information.

Other data in this book was based on Samuel Guldin's diary discovered in the Bern (Switzerland) Archives in 1897. A Swiss minister who was exiled from Switzerland, Guldin kept an excellent descriptive diary published in October 1960 and April 1961 in the *Mennonite Research Journal.*

The Hans Herr House was bought in 1969 by the Lancaster Mennonite Conference Historical Society and restored in the 1970s. It is open for tours from Monday through Saturday from 9:00 a.m. to 4:00 p.m. The homestead includes a blacksmith shop and a museum.

Christian Herr's original Bible is housed at the Hans Herr House, as is also Martin Mylin's songbook. Benedict Brechbühl's Bible is housed at the new library at Fairmount Rest Home. Hans Herr's *Ausbund* can be seen at the Amish Historical Library at Aylmer, Ontario, Canada.

Plans are to continue this story, Lord willing, in a future book tracing Christian Herr's daughter, Barbrara and her marriage to David Martin of Weberdahl/Weaverland.

We owe a debt of gratitude to many who helped in this book: to John Ruth for editing suggestions and corrections; to our daughter-in-law Anita (Shirk) Burkholder for the artwork; as well as all the typists and editors who worked with us. Enos and I are Old Order Mennonite (Groffdale Conference), and have four children: Ina, Ethan, Orpha, and Beulah, who all have an interest in history. Our handicapped daughter, Julia, passed away in 1997.

This book was written in the hope that it may bring a deeper appreciation of our rich spiritual heritage. For those who are interested in digging deeper, the following is a small selection of books (all available at Masthof Bookstore, 219 Mill Road, Morgantown, PA 19543; e-mail: mast@masthof.com:

Bender, Harold S. and C. Henry Smith. *Mennonites and Their Heritage, A Handbook of Mennonite History and Belief.* Scottdale, Pa.: Herald Press, 1986. 148pp. $4.75.

Blank, Ben S. *The Amazing Story of the Ausbund.* Author, 2001. 120pp. $10.00.

Confession of Faith in a Mennonite Perspective. Scottdale, Pa.: Herald Press, 1996. 112pp. $4.95.

Gratz, Delbert L. *Bernese Anabaptists and Their American Descendants.* Morgantown, Pa.: Masthof Press, 1994. 219pp. illus. hardcover. index. $18.95.

Guth, Hermann and Gertrud Guth and J. Lemar and Lois Ann Mast. *Palatine Mennonite Census Lists, 1664-1793.* Morgantown, Pa.: Masthof Press, 1987. 116pp. illus. index. $12.50.

Herr, Theodore. *Genealogical Record of Reverend Hans Herr and His Direct Lineal Descendants.* Lancaster, Pa.: LMHS, 1994. $40.00.

Jackson, Dave and Neta. *On Fire For Christ: Storries of Anabaptist Martyrs Retold From Martyrs Mirror.* Scottdale, Pa.: Herald Press, 1989. 184pp. $10.99.

Kauffman, John. *Anabaptist Letters From 1635 to 1645: Translation From the Ausbund.* Martha K. Coffman, 1994. 29pp. $3.00.

Kreider, Robert S. and John S. Oyer. *Mirror of the Martyrs.* Intercourse, Pa.: Good Books, 1990. 96pp. illus. $9.95.

Ruth, John L. *The Earth is the Lord's, A Narrative History of the Lancaster Mennonite Conference.* Scottdale, Pa.: Herald Press, 2001. 1,390pp. illus. hardcover. index. $65.00.

Schlabach, Verna. *Anabaptist Timeline.* 10"x25" chart. illus. $4.95.

The Swiss Anabaptists, A Brief Summary of Their History and Beliefs. Ephrata, Pa.: Eastern Mennonite Pub., 1990. 121pp. $6.50.

van Braght, Thieleman J. *Martyrs Mirror.* Scottdale, Pa.: Herald Press, 1938. 1,1458pp. illus. $37.50.

Wenger, Samuel S. *The Wenger Book.* Pennsylvania German Heritage History, Inc., 1978. 2 vols. 1,248pp. and 480pp. illus. hardcover. index. $49.50.

- Mabel Burkholder, Author
Fleetwood, Pennsylvania
October 2002